The Maldive Chronicles

and Other Stories

PAJ FictionContemporary

For information, write to PAJ Publications, 325 Spring Street, Suite 318, New York, N.Y. 10013.

Library of Congress Cataloging in Publication Data
The Maldive Chronicles: Stories by Kenneth Bernard
Library of Congress Catalog Card No.: 87-81204
ISBN: 1-55554-019-8

Printed in the United States of America

Publication of this book has been made possible in part by grants received from the National Endowment for the Arts, Washington, D.C., a federal agency, and the New York State Council on the Arts.

The Maldive Chronicles

stories by

Kenneth Bernard

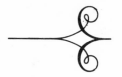

PAJ Publications
New York

Acknowledgements

These stories have appeared in the following periodicals, texts, and anthologies:

American Review: "King Kong: A Meditation," "Sister Francetta and the Pig Baby."
Bennington Review: "The Girl Who Might or Might Not Have Read Sartre."
Dialogue: "The Whitman Lesson."
Fiction International: "The Films of R. Nixon," "Question and Answer."
Harper's: "The Woman Who Thought She Was Beautiful."
Iowa Review: "Teddy and I Go Kong."
Grand Street: "Bird-Watching," "Fox-Trot and Other Matters," "Morsels," "Epistemology on the March," "Preparations," "Rescheduling."
Last Night's Stranger, ed. Pat Rotter (New York, 1982): "Dirty Old Man."
Minnesota Review: The Maldive Chronicles.
Response: A Contemporary Jewish Review: "Walking."
2 Plus 2 (Switzerland): "George Washington's Birthday."

Contents

The Maldive Chronicles

and

Other Stories

for Elaine

Question and Answer

I HAVE ON OCCASION BEEN ASKED TO READ MY FICTIONAL formulations. On the whole, I do not mind. If I am paid, of course, I view the occasion with a certain business detachment. I am usually nervous before, warm up during the reading (although never enough to be demonstrative), and relax in the question and answer period. In this last part, I am responsible for nothing. I can always answer truthfully I don't know. And in other matters (i.e., where I appear to have an answer), who can really argue? Best of all I like questions about what kind of pen or pencil I use, what paper or pad, when do I write, how much is autobiographical (practically nothing: an admittedly cagey answer), do I write on a desk or table, do I drink or eat, and especially *persona*. *Persona* thrills me to my core. Sometimes there is an obviously hostile questioner. There is a sneer, a condescension in his voice. He clearly thinks me stupid and untalented, or not enough talented to merit the present gathering (to which he has so conspicuously come). Actually, I can't remember the last time I had such an interlocutor; people are generally quite polite. But I do *think* about him a lot (it's never a she). And I spend a fair amount of time answering this type. For example:

Thank you, sir. I can't satisfy you entirely. It is clear to me you are rude. You are also arrogant and therefore ignorant; angry, vain, sneering, condescending, and probably untalented and envious. In other words, if you don't beat your mother, wife, child, or pet, you are probably guilty of some similarly unacceptable behavior, nameless and hidden though it may be. I cannot deal with all that. That is your problem. As to the question itself, may I rephrase it more clearly for you? Most of what you ask you have answered in the form of your question. That is, your formulation is tautological and self-serving; it eliminates almost all possibilities except those

3

which will render me a scoundrel or worse. What, then, is legitimately left? What is left is "Why?" or, more elaborately, "Why did I write such a story, let alone read it?" The answer is I don't know. I have some ideas, but we both know they will not be the whole story, perhaps none of it. Nothing is ever the whole story, and most things are usually totally *other* stories, if I make myself clear. It might be fun to give these ideas anyway, but only if we keep in mind it is merely fun, without obligation or privilege. Who could know or say why I wrote and/or read such a story? It clearly comes from the mystery of me to the mystery of you and takes place in the infinite complicated mystery of life. Thus, even in reformulation, your question is always a trick question, because it is, as I say, a question without a true answer. A better one would be, for example, on what day of the week did I begin the story or how many times did I revise it or did I write initially on a yellow legal pad, lined or unlined white paper, or a notebook. And even the middle question here must be withdrawn because we do not know what actually constitutes revision. If I change one word, is it a revision? You say no. But I think we must admit that what word it is and where matters a great deal. That is, it *could* be a revision, say *Mustela putorius* for polecat or *Phallus impudicus* for stinkhorn. To say, however, that a retyping of any changes is a revision is too categorical. If each time I go over the pieces and change one detail is a revision, there might be hundreds of revisions, and dozens more as I type. Further, the sequence and significance of such "revisions" are probably lost forever; no one, certainly not I, can ever know in what order I did them or why. I am not a bookkeeper. Monday I change this word, Tuesday I change that word, the following Friday, after eating a ham sandwich, I go back and change still three other words, and so on. What is the point of it all, except, possibly, to bemoan lost worlds (not in itself, I admit, a bad idea necessarily)? All I can say is that I revise and that I do it with a thick pen. The thick pen is very real. That leaves the other questions. To which I say: I don't remember on what day of the week I began this particular story, but if I looked up my original draft I could find out; and I prefer to do my first drafts on yellow legal pads without

4

too much space between the lines and with a perforated top so that I can easily rip out pages. Thereafter I type my versions double space and write in changes between the lines, in the margins, and on the backs of the sheets. I am perfectly happy to tell you this. I think it reveals something about me and my work and satisfies a legitimate curiosity. In these matters we have, I think, considerable communication. Otherwise, we are just being fools, playing games, filling in time. If I wanted to know something about you, for example, I would ask your shoe size or what color underwear you have on or exactly how much money is in your wallet. I hope you understand what I am saying. I am sorry you're leaving. And I'm sorry to see that you are using crutches. I hope it is nothing permanent or painful. You should have sat at the end of the row. I shall be happy to answer any other questions you may have. Good luck, sir.

Epistemology on the March

I HAVE A FRIEND, A PHILOSOPHER, WHO CLAIMS TO BE IN THE analytic tradition. And for all I know, this is so. But it is not of overriding interest to me. In stature he is not diminutive, but he is most certainly not Wagnerian either. He spends a great deal of time skittering along the aisle outside his office, chuckling, rubbing his apocalyptic hands, gossiping, playing sly little word games, tyrannizing the secretaries, and skirting lunacy. Hermeneutics, he says, is on the wrong track. Nothing is thinkable, he says, without foundations. His own patch is medical ethics, and we have many a chuckle over the conundrums of the health-related spheres, kidney machines and such. As a sideline he conjures up grants for conferences and symposia, and together we work up panel titles like "Are Profit-Makers More Virile?" to pull in the crowd. I try, now and then, to convince him that philosophers, like physicists, believe quite incorrectly that they have the world by the tail, that they are all Napoleons in closets. This entertains him enormously. Further, I tell him that foundationalism is sexist, that all women are natural hermeneuticists, that a recent survey of analytic philosophers revealed that they are on the whole shorter than hermeneuticists, Faustian in temperament, and vastly tolerated and indulged by their wives. He will have none of it. I have tried to interest him in animal rights. He is sympathetic but not interested, although we had one jolly discussion about interspecies organ banks for ailing baboons.

Despite his Napoleonic and Faustian delusions, he is quite charming, industrious, and bright. He laughs often in spite of himself, blushes easily, and enjoys, more than he admits, the quirkiness of life. But we do not see eye to eye. For example, I believe that if we were to recite the theory of the hydrogen bomb in Greek while standing on our heads spitting grape seeds we might well discover that it is also a theory about how to turn rabbits into toads, to which the explosion of hydrogen bombs would be merely a footnote. Dangerous nonsense, he says, quack relativism. It doesn't help that a colleague of his of less epistemological persuasion wears pink shorts to his summer logic classes.

Simmering within his breast there is also a political radical, a Kropotkin of the breakfast table. He was quite upset recently over the prospect of buying a ninety-thousand-dollar summer house, which he planned, except for a room for him and his wife, a professional, to rent to students. Like a nearby chairman who is billed as a Trotskyite, he longs passionately for a revolution of rights, a perfect and brotherly equity on earth. To be sure, his hands have not yet been awash with blood; he has not seen the spattering of flesh. Nor has he touched the cold flesh of a loved one, dead in a noble cause. He has not, as we say, been tested by fire. When I suggest that dialogue is all, or nearly all, he imperiously disagrees. There are times, he says, when it is necessary to *act*. He has me there. I agree. But *when*? When does one, so to speak, abandon one's medical ethics? When is it *proper* to overlook one person's suffering and death for another's? Obviously it takes great epistemological security to be efficiently radical, or to arbitrate among the suffering and downtrodden. A *code* of justice or of medical ethics has a fine sound, until one hears the chains and screams. One day I told him he had a definite epistemological strut. He positively barked with pleasure. All such phrases delight him. The hermeneutic slouch, or glide. The Teutonic thrust. Tripping the phenomenological fantastic. From world beating to wife beating. The tooth of teleology. We have great fun.

Yet I cannot avoid the occasional image of his eye beating down at me along a gun barrel. "Wait, wait, Izzie, can't we talk?" "No more talk," he says; "tomorrow is here." "Epistemology!" I cry. "Bang," he smiles, his bicornuate helmet tipping a little. And everything goes black.

The Girl Who Might or Might Not Have Read Sartre

I ONCE KNEW A GIRL WHO READ SARTRE. OR AT LEAST SO I WAS told. And it was the making of her. Before, she had been pretty and bright, wrote well, and had a future. After, she was still pretty for a while, continued to be bright, but she exchanged her future for an enormously complex present which seemed to exist only to feed an increasingly grotesque past. Her name was Madeline. When I first met her I knew she was bright, but she seemed vacant. I could not, for example, imagine her in love. And at times I wondered whether her clarity of mind might not be derivative. She knew she was brighter than I, but she knew it quietly, politely. She was a lady. Oddly, even years later, long after she had committed herself to something, when she looked battered and older than she was, she still seemed a lady. At least with me. Perhaps because I had been her teacher. And I was grateful for that quality, that deference. Otherwise I would have been frightened, vulnerable. For after all, she came to know things I did not, could or would not. She was also, as I say, pretty, and attracted to me. I don't think I could have dealt with her proposals. Nevertheless, I gather she must have made them somehow. I feel the weight of them, whatever they were, and the weight of my having missed them. Why else would she have come back? And to me?

The first time, several years after she graduated, was to clarify something in her record. "Ah. You are going to graduate school, then?" I said. "Perhaps," she answered. "I'm applying for a teaching job." I was disappointed. She was better than a mere teaching job. "Are you married?" I asked. "No," she said, "we're not married." I didn't ask her why. Or whom. I presumed it was the same young man she had taken up with while an undergraduate. A piece of information that had, at the time, disturbed me. She had seemed too fine, too remote and poised, for an affair, an engagement of the flesh. Yet it must have been so. The young man was pleasant but not as bright as she. He had, without much talent, fancied himself a writer. He was, I remember being told, good-hearted. "So things are going well?" I said. She paused before she spoke. "Yes. Things are going well." I thought of her pause a long time after. And I pondered her words. I regretted that I had not asked her what *he* was doing.

He must have been doing something, for when next I heard of her she had two children. But she was still unmarried. She obviously had made decisions. When she came in again it was not specifically to see me, but with a friend who was seeing someone else. "How are you?" I said. "Fine," she answered, and smiled. But she was not fine. She was missing a tooth in the front of her mouth. She was no longer a girl, but a woman, a woman not yet middle-aged, but not young either. Her clothes were neat but shabby. I pitied her, and she saw that I pitied her. Her expression did not change, but her eyes communicated amusement, perhaps even contempt. "And is Edwin writing?" I tried to recover. "He's driving a cab," she said. Then she relented and gave me her full smile, looking even older. "And how are *you* doing?" she said. "The same," I answered, "the same as usual. I never change." "Yes. Coming here is like coming home," she said. It was an odd statement, a disconcerting one. Was I like a father to her? I watched her leave. There was nothing attractive, nothing feminine or stirring about her. Her body seemed far too hidden, although I knew it must be there. She was twenty-six, nearly twenty-seven. I spoke to the man her friend had seen and found out that Madeline was a waitress, that Edwin was sometimes unfaithful, that they had no intention of getting married, that the children, a boy and a girl, were six and four, that they lived in a small apartment in a drab section of Brooklyn. But what did they say to each other? I wondered. I felt vaguely stupid and unconnected with life, although in fact I was married, published, and a parent. I also felt I had let her down.

Officially I saw her only once more, although I have several times thought I passed near her in the street, in the subways, perhaps in a store. It was nearly eight years later. I would not have known her had she not spoken. It was in a post office. I immediately wondered whether she was writing, and just as immediately knew she was not. She was not much heavier, but much older. She seemed to know my questions. "Still two children, still Edwin, still unmarried," she said, and smiled at me. I was certain her teeth were false. "He's teaching junior high school now and likes it very much." "Wonderful," I said, "and how are *you*?" I must have put meaning into my question because she answered, "I'm still very fine," as if in response to some unspoken dialogue. We stood there awkwardly a few seconds. I knew she was waiting, knew she had chosen not to leave. "You've...had a very interesting life," I said, and immediately blushed. She appeared not to notice and very seriously said to me, "Yes. I have. Have you?" "I hope so," I laughed. "I'm waiting for someone to tell me." She said nothing. I wondered again whether she had in fact written those most literate papers years ago. It occurred to me that she could still have children if she wished. "Give my regards to Edwin," I said, "He speaks of you often," she said. "He enjoyed your course very much." But he never took my course, I nearly blurted, and then realized he probably had, and I had forgotten. Someone once told me he was of medium height and had blond hair. I could not visualize him. "Are you still waitressing?" I asked. "Yes. We need the money." "Don't we all." "I must go," she said. "Goodbye." I shook her hand. It was not as rough as I expected. "Good luck," I said. She said nothing, but smiled. And left. Left. Passionately I wondered what her hours were, and where, why she had lost her teeth, what she read, if anything, why she lived in Brooklyn, what she really felt about Edwin and whether he was still sometimes unfaithful, how many clothes she had, what her children were named, whether she used perfume, the size of her shoe, how many rooms they lived in and how clean, what they watched on television at night, and a thousand other things. I never found out about any of them. But I often hope, sometimes fervently, that I am living an interesting life, and that she approves of it.

The Woman
Who Thought She Was Beautiful

THE AUTUMN I FIRST KNEW HER SHE HAD TURNED TWENTY-
one. Almost the first thing she said to me was, "I am beautiful. Are
you not struck by it?" I smiled at her audacity and replied indeed, I
was, although it had happened only the moment she said it. The *first*
thing she had said to me was a quotation: "'Pain and love,'" she
recited, "'—the whole of life, in short—cannot be looked upon as a
disease because they make us suffer.' Svevo, *Confessions of Zeno*.
Don't you agree?" She had the gift of immediate intimacy, and
added that just the previous night she had taken her first lover, and
didn't it make a difference? "In what?" I answered her seriously.
"My allure," she said, and I laughed. "You're very rude," she pouted,
and left me. It was true. I had laughed too loudly. I realized now that
it was out of jealousy of that first lover and anger at her for telling
me. I also realize that in some wholly unaccountable way I had been
chosen to try for the position of second lover. But I, too, was young.

When I saw her again she was five years older, and knew more.
She came to me as if we had spoken only yesterday. "And have you
read Svevo yet?" she asked. And followed it quickly with "You were
a fool, you know." I blushed, and muttered that I was married. She
laughed, just a shade too loudly. "And if you were not?" Like an
idiot, I laughed too. "You know," she said, "I married him, that first
one. Oh, not right away. There were others. And it was a mistake.
He was weak. He thought he was a master because I gave myself to
him. Purely out of joy. But he was not. He gave no joy *back*. You
came a day too late. Do you play tennis?" Her lips were the loveliest
I have ever seen, and I stared at them. "Am I still beautiful?" she
asked. I nodded. "Yes," she said, "I thought you would think so. My
son is three." "Mine is two," I said, and cursed myself. There was a
pause. "I'm sure," she said, "you're a lovely father. And do read
Svevo soon. He is quite mad." It was about as pleasant a dismissal as

I could expect. I did not play tennis.

Sixteen years later, while Christmas shopping, we met again. "Do you believe in Santa Claus?" she said. I answered no, and knew that either answer was wrong. "I am married again," she confessed. "Have you prospered?" "Yes," I answered, "I have done well." She wore a fur-trimmed coat. Beneath it I felt her warm body. "Would you like to ask me something?" she said. I hesitated, feeling guilty for staring at her lips rather than her eyes. "How is your son?" I asked. "You are remarkable," she replied. "You must come to my funeral someday." "Will it be soon, do you know?" "*Hypocrite*," she said, giving it the French intonation, and turned to leave. "Wait," I called. She turned and waited, but gave me nothing. She would not compromise me. "I really must go," she said finally. "I'm sorry I was rude," I said. She turned and left. In my head I said, "Wait. You are still beautiful. Where are you staying? May I come?" And then I finished my shopping.

It turned out that I did go to her funeral. Once, in the interval, I had seen her in a canoe, and she had waved, and looked at me until she was out of sight. Several other times I had the feeling that I had just missed her, that only a moment or two before she had stood where I was. It was a small funeral, and people, though discreet, were surprised to see me. Their eyes said, "Was *he* one of them?" But I was nearly old, although I did not know it, and the curiosity was historical. I was also a widower, with grown children, to whom a certain deference was due. A skiing accident, they said. Can you imagine, at her age, still the most difficult runs. Still—yes, I understood. I looked at her. She was still beautiful. She looked younger than she must have been, no older, actually, than she had looked in the canoe. It had rained that afternoon, and I had waited for the canoe to return. But it had not; they had found shelter by the river. I had drunk a lot of tea, and my wife had said, "Are you well? Are you getting a chill?" I wanted to bend over and kiss her lips, for a brief moment to kiss them savagely. But I did not. I should have cried and made a fool of myself. "She is very lovely, is she not?" said a very old man, who I later found out was her third husband. "Yes," I answered, "very beautiful." *But not, I thought, as* beautiful as she might have been! And I could not stop myself. I wept by her coffin. The old man put his hand on my arm. "We all loved her," he said, "but perhaps not enough."

King Kong: A Meditation

TARZAN AND KONG

IT IS LOGICAL THAT HAVING WRITTEN AT SOME LEGNTH ON King Kong I should turn to Tarzan of the Apes. There are many striking parallels. For example, their native habitat is jungle. Further, Tarzan, like Kong, seems unable to find his generative organ, or, if he has found it, seems equally unable to divine its function. Hence in both cases a good deal of sublimated sexuality in the form of encounters with wild beasts. (A good question here is, how would Tarzan and Kong have gotten along? Perhaps they would have established what one critic has described as an innocent homosexual relationship. Can you imagine, for example, Kong and Tarzan floating down the Mississippi on a raft, sharing a perfect trust and understanding as well as naked moonlit swims under the stars?) But all this is really by the way, though not without a certain interest. What makes Tarzan of the Apes peculiarly interesting to me at the moment is his faculty of speech. Kong, for all his expressiveness, for all his frustrated flooding at the gates of articulation, is a dumb brute, whereas Tarzan has given utterance to several of our civilization's notable word and vowel configurations.

Take "HUNGAWA!" for example. (One is reminded, perhaps, of Eliot's "Hakagawa.") This is almost invariably the directive Tarzan gives to an elephant when a situation is critical. Miles off (down or up river), a young, frightened woman is about to be ripped into four pieces by bent saplings as lascivious sweating savages leer at her. (It is really very stupid of them, since all they can do afterwards is eat her.) But crashing through the bush on the tide of "HUNGAWA!" come Tarzan and his elephant (or sometimes elephants). She will be saved (though not won); the savages will scatter in jabbering

14

fear as their meager huts are crushed by an elephant's foot. It would be a mistake, of course, to think that "HUNGAWA!" meant only "Hurry!" Sometimes it means "Push." And sometimes "Gather ye (elephants, beasts of the jungle, et cetera) round." On at least one occasion it was addressed to a lion and meant, roughly, "Cut it out! Behave yourself!" Upon (repeated) which, the lion slunk off. In other words, context and tone (even repetition) are everything. One constant, though, is the imperative, the exclamatory. Urgency and command are always there. It is man's Ur-*cri* for crisis—in which man still feels the power to control. There would be something laughable in the businessman rushing by taxi to catch his train shouting "HUNGAWA!" (The cab driver would fix his wagon promptly.) But how appropriate for the astronaut at blast-off to scream "HUNGAWA!" to the TV audience. What a thrilling link of old and new.

Another notable expression of Tarzan's is the discovery, "Me Tarzan, you Jane." This is the quintessential boy meets girl. With the reservation that Tarzan does not know the generative function of his penis. It is quite likely that Jane does not either; otherwise she would learn to use "HUNGAWA!" for her own end. A horrendous scene would be Jane screaming "HUNGAWA!" like a fishwife at Tarzan and Tarzan scratching his head in befuddlement, as did Kong when he held the screaming blonde maiden in his fist for the first time. (Why is she screaming? What does she think I will do to her?) But Jane does not know about his penis. That is why she spends so much time swimming. But her relationship to elephants is significantly different from his. She obviously gets a different feeling from riding them than does Tarzan. It is not blatantly sexual, but quite clearly we would see nothing wrong with grape juice dripping down her chin while astride an elephant. Tarzan, on the other hand, never masturbates. He simply does not know it. Yet, contradictorily, we feel he disapproves of it (whatever it is), and speaks harshly to his household chimps when he catches them at it. Jane is probably more permissive.* This slight difference in

---

*We must also bear in mind, I think, that Jane is a barbarian American and Tarzan an Englishman, Lord Greystoke, to be precise. In whatever he does, there is a "natural

15

their natures would undoubtedly have pushed them to some domestic crisis in which Tarzan could not have shouted "HUN-GAWA!" There would ultimately have to be a limit to the amount of swimming Jane could take, or flowers in her hair (what a clever game, that), or pineapple stuffed in her mouth, or tandem swinging through the trees. They are saved from this crisis by the discovery of Boy in the jungle. They have fulfilled the Biblical injunction and multiplied. Yet one senses some artificiality in all this. For example, "Me Tarzan, you Jane, him Boy" clearly does not have the epic rightness of the shorter phrase. Equally clearly, some accommodation has been made. And in this accommodation we have one of those mirror instances in which we see ourselves naked, so to speak. Because it is all right with us. We are content to have them find Boy in an overgrown cabbage patch. We *want* Jane to go on swimming and Tarzan to go on fighting crocodiles and renegade lions. Just as we do not want Kong to violate that blonde maiden, so too we do not want Tarzan to share carnal knowledge with Jane. Yet at the same time these are precisely what we do want. We want Kong to grow big and approach the blonde maiden with bloodshot, lustful eyes. Similarly, one day when Jane has arisen dripping from her swim and is awaiting her flower in the hair, we want Tarzan to rip off her garment and shout "HUNGAWA!" The elephants would undoubtedly come running but would not necessarily be a problem. Boy, in this event, would become the jungle's first juvenile delinquent; his reversion to abandonment would be too much after reigning as Tarzan's heir apparent. Perhaps he would seek his real father. Perhaps he would destroy Tarzan and Jane's first genital child. In sum, civilization would ensue. But this is not what happens. The balance is kept. Paradise is not lost. We have our cake and eat it, too, for in fantasy we penetrate the blonde maiden and Jane, are ravished by the vision of innocence outrageously, stupendously lost. Tarzan or Kong with erections are unthinkable,

---

outcropping of many generations of fine breeding, an hereditary instinct of graciousness which a lifetime of uncouth and savage training and environment could not eradicate" (*Tarzan of the Apes*, Chapter XX). Thus, though he may eat the raw meat of a lion he has just killed, his erections must in no way intrude, that is, rattle the teacups. There is also, perhaps, just a *schmeck* of Anglophobia in having Jane, whose breeding is, after all, only acquired, civilize the apelike English lord.

but somewhere in the furry depth, beneath that loincloth, they *lurk*, waiting to spring to life at our call. And at that moment, civilization will destroy itself, for we could not, in our finitude, in our infantilism, stand that much joy. We would go mad with it and run raging in the streets. Kong, because in effect he *wants* his erection, must be destroyed. Tarzan, the docile one, we allow to live. "HUNGAWA!" is no fit comparison for Kong's shrieks of rage on the Empire State Building as bullets pour into him. It is the pain and anger of all men in their betrayal. Deep within us we all cry out for the blonde maiden to violate, to plunge the very Empire State into her and achieve orgasm with the cosmos. But we do not, we cannot. We must content ourselves with a "HUNGAWA!" to the elephants and the lions, while Jane, sleek and wet (but ever clothed) with the lily-studded water, swims ever away, even as we join her and swim down, down into misty depths.

HOW BIG IS KONG'S PENIS?

In a recent meditation on King Kong and Tarzan of the Apes, I wrote the following: "We want Kong to grow big and approach the blonde maiden with bloodshot, lustful eyes." There are several interesting problems here. For example, Fay Wray, the blonde maiden, who is to say she is a maiden? (Actually, she is not even blonde.) When found by the impresario Carl Denham and taken to a waterfront café (read *dive*) she is alone and starving. She is down on her luck. She has come upon *bad times*. Denham clearly wants someone with nothing more to lose, and when he sees her there is a flash, or burst, of recognition. The cards, we can say, are pretty heavily stacked against maidenhood. Yet, surprisingly, Fay Wray *is* a maiden, which gives this adventure much of its fairy-tale quality. We know this from a scene that is not (and could not be) in the movie but which obviously had to take place. For years the island savages have been giving maidens to Kong. They are not going to break with tradition simply because Fay Wray is white. The whiteness is merely an added spice, or sauce. She must be maiden *and* white. The scene not included in the movie is that wherein the

17

chief, the elders, and the midwives of the tribe examine a naked Fay Wray gynecologically. As all those black fingers probe and poke Fay Wray, she must be thinking that nothing can be worse than this, just as in the waterfront café she had thought she could sink no lower. How wrong she was and is. This limit to her imagination makes Kong's initial appearance all the more devastating. Kong is literally *beyond her wildest imaginings*. It is worth noting that Fay's first vision of Kong is an (arch) typical bride's first night fantasy of her husband. When Kong appears, Fay Wray is severed forever from the civilization that bred her. The unspeakable has become life. If her mind has not already been sprung by the savages' examination of her virgin body, it surely is now. She will never be the same. In any event, it is clear that the savages would not have offered her to Kong had they not been assured of her maidenhood. We could also adduce as proof the evidence of the first mate's love for her: his instinct would not have failed him: no *used* woman (and he surely knew them) could have aroused him to a pure love. But this is superfluous; the anthropological inference is conclusive enough.

A second interesting point in the quotation is the oblique reference to Kong's penis in the phrase "to grow big." Exactly how big *is* Kong's penis? It is a matter of monumental cultural and psychological interest. And a great mystery: for *Kong's penis is never shown; he is no common monkey in the zoo.* (Its absence, of course, is the reason why it is dreamed about so much.) It is quite possible that Denham, before he leaves the island with Kong, emasculates him (in another unfilmed episode)* to assure his docility later on. (An interesting question here is, if this is so, what did the savages do with it or them? There is quite possibly an interesting totemic myth buried here.) That might well explain Kong's interest in the Empire State Building later on. Realizing that he is without his penis or its generative power (in fact or in his mind—for his defeat and humiliation at Denham's hands may well have resulted in a psychological emasculation, a temporary impotence), and that there is something he cannot do with Fay Wray without it, he seeks

---

*Dare I suggest how admirable this scene, as well as the earlier one between Fay Wray and the savages, would be, today, in Technicolor or VistaVision?

to attach another penis to himself. Here his ape brain reveals itself. (Question: Does Fay Wray have any inkling of what Kong intends? Probably, though only an inkling. Kong constantly shatters the limits of her nightmares. He plunges her from one insanity into another—but who is to say that heaven itself is not awaiting her within that final, absolute, insanity?) If this is so, we might well accuse Kong of certain immodesty. A penis (even erect) the size of the Empire State Building? But we cannot be sure, for we have never seen it. There is, however, some slight indirect evidence of size. When Kong storms the walls that separate him from the savages, seeking his stolen maiden, with what does he batter them? It is definitely a possibility. But still, not Empire State dimension, not even the upper dome. We can only put *that* gesture down to a rage beyond all reason.

Which still leaves us with the problem of Kong's penis. There is, of course, the peculiar behavior of Kong from the beginning. He obviously does not ravish Fay Wray immediately. He is not even sexually curious about her. How are we to explain his early *playfulness* with her and his later *libidinous determination*? (He has not chosen the Empire State idly.) The answer, I think, is to be found in his age. Kong, up through his island adventures with Fay, is a child. He sees her merely as a new and unusual plaything. (What has happened to his earlier playthings is problematical. As I have indicated elsewhere, I lean toward the idea that he ate them.) But, during his voyage to America (possibly even just before the voyage, if we bear the wall-battering in mind), he arrives at puberty, and in America he is a young adult—hence his altered interest in Fay. But now there is no penis or penis power from which to effect his end. Part of his problem (assuming Denham's butchery, which we need not) is that he very likely has little recollection of his penis and what its varying aspects were. (Question: *Did* Kong ever masturbate?) He is also unsettled from the sea voyage, the gas, and the total change in environment. Hence his berserk casting about for a substitute.

But *we* need not be equally at sea. A simple scientific approach will give us at least a reasonable working hypothesis. One of Kong's first destructive acts in the New World is the wrecking of an elevated train and its track. The track is about twenty feet off the ground and reaches Kong's shoulders. Kong therefore must be about twenty-four feet tall. Further, we can usually count on a six-foot man having a three-inch inert and six-inch erect penis. Assuming the validity of comparative anatomy, we can say therefore that Kong's penis would be twelve inches inert and twenty-four inches, or two feet, erect. And this is a startling fact. Because it really doesn't seem so very big. Even its fatness would not increase its shock impact, for the fatter it is, the *shorter* it would seem. Possibly it is some horrendous blue or purple, or pointed, or wickedly curved—but even these would have limited shock value. A more experienced woman than Fay might even, *momentarily and in spite of herself*, entertain the thought of what it would be like. So we are left with this fact: that the penis Kong ought to have is insufficient to cause the terror and anxiety he inspires. Therefore the penis Kong has is the one he *ought not* to have. Of course one can suggest that the horror of Kong is in his size *in general*, that is, a twenty-four-foot ape—but only to reject it. For the entire drama of Kong is not built around his general size or destructiveness but around his relationship with Fay Wray. And the entire point of this relationship is that it is male and female and that it aspires to the condition of consummation! The only question—and it harbors an anxiety that reaches into the very depth of our civilization—is *When?* When will Kong's twenty-four-inch erect penis penetrate the white and virgin (and quivering) body of Fay Wray? And there, of course, we have the solution. It is easily conceivable that in these circumstances some people, perhaps many, would say, "Who cares?" Precisely. Twenty-four inches is not *that* awe-inspiring. But people say no such thing. *It is obvious that Kong must exceed the estimates of comparative anatomy to inspire the universal dread that he does.*

Kong's penis, therefore, is at least six feet inert and twelve feet erect (or seventy-two and one hundred and forty-four inches respectively). In a state of sexual excitement it very likely rises over his head. *That* would certainly explain the battering at the savages' wall, and it certainly explains the terror in New York City's streets:

a twenty-four-foot ape with a twelve-foot erection stalking the streets for this woman. The blasé mode is simply not possible in the face of such a Kong. No experience is equal to it. There is no room for wonder, only fear. And so, in the end, when Kong, half-crazed by bullets and frustrations he has experienced, identifies sexually with the Empire State Building, he is not, after all, being immodest. He has sought only what all true lovers seek, in the only way that he could. He has brought his love to the threshold of his love and valiantly persevered to his last desperate breath. Dazed beyond recall, so near and yet so far, he loosens his grip, his fingers slip. No longer can he guide his newfound power into her. Kong cannot live erect in the New World. And uttering a last terrifying cry from within his battered heart (who will ever forget it?), he falls, falls ever so far, perhaps momentarily remembering the lushness of his island paradise, wet from dew in the silent and foggy primeval morning, falls to his cold and concrete death. In truth, as Carl Denham mutters, Fay Wray hath killed the beast.

THE MIND AND THE HEART OF FAY WRAY

It is clear to me that far too little attention has been paid to Fay Wray, the love of King Kong. Not only is her experience terrifying and transcendental (*sublime*, as Burke would have it), but it is also not lost on her. When Kong dies, Fay Wray knows that no other lover in her life will be equal to him. She may not be able to articulate the changes that have placed her beyond merely human experiences, but she has absorbed them, she is alive and (psychologically) whole: she has confronted King Kong and received his blessing among an alien breed. She will henceforth dwell among them but not be *of* them. Had she experienced sexual union with Kong, she would (also) have been omnipotent and omniscient. In this essay I should like to discuss several aspects of her psychopsychical journey.

The Disappearing Bottom

When we first encounter Fay Wray, she is the most ordinary of women, except in one respect. She has fallen down the socio-economic ladder. Her attitude at this point is that little, if anything, worse can happen to her. She has touched bottom. What makes her different from other girls is that instead of laughing at Carl Denham's crackpot offer she eagerly accepts it. This decision is focal: all things come from it. It is a decision that reflects deeply on her character. However, this decision is also the beginning of a series of false states of mind. For at the moment Fay Wray decides in favor of Denham's proposal, she thinks that she is rising from the bottom. In fact, the bottom has just dropped, and she is falling further. She reaches the new bottom when the island savages seize her (we shall examine this in detail later). For now we can say that once more Fay Wray thinks nothing could be worse, but in fact the bottom has again dropped and she is falling. (It is part of Fay's destiny always to have her worst expectations exceeded.) She reaches a new low when, tied to the stake outside the savages' protective barrier, she hears and then sees King Kong for the first time. At this point, being down and out in a waterfront café must seem like heaven to her. Although she is conscious here of things being worse than they were with the savages, she knows that they are probably going to get still worse when Kong actually reaches her. Death, of course, will be the absolute bottom, and she cannot face it; she faints. When she comes to, she realizes that Kong perhaps has other ideas, and once more the bottom has dropped: she now faces a fate worse than death.* She exists in this extreme anxiety until she is rescued. Again the feeling of rising from the bottom. Then Kong returns for her (some brief anxiety), is subdued by Denham, and carried to the New World. Fay Wray has, apparently, reached *the* bottom and come back to tell the tale. Although she must undoubtedly be psychologically wary, she is relieved, she relaxes, she feels it is all over. She is about to resume

---

*Or, to be more correct, cf. E.R. Burroughs' *Tarzan of the Apes*, Chapter XIX, when Terkoz, the deposed ape leader, bends Jane Porter to his "awful fangs": "But ere they touched that fair skin another mood claimed the anthropoid. The tribe had kept his women. He must find others to replace them. This hairless white ape would be the first of his new household, and so he threw her roughly across his broad hairy shoulders and leaped back into the trees, bearing Jane Porter away toward *a fate a thousand times worse than death*." [my italics]

22

her former life, but on a higher socioeconomic plane. And then the bottom drops again: Kong escapes, finds her, and takes her to the top of the Empire State building.

Kong and the Empire State Building: the meeting of two giants. (Which one will get Fay?) Kong is on the verge of a great symbolic act. He will ram the Empire State into Fay as if it were (as in a sense it is) his very own. It is a desperate, noble, futile, tragic attempt on a par with Ahab's defiance of his finitude. But Ahab's attempt, while broadly human, is entirely personal (monomaniacal, as his first mate realizes). Kong's attempt is personal, but it is also grandly humanitarian, an attempt to reunite two worlds God never meant to be separate. However, it is too late. Any progeny of such a union could be only monstrous (or totally holy, which would be monstrous). The distance is too great; time has become too irrevocable. Here Kong seems not so much apelike as he does innocent. Here we take him most to our hearts. He is, like Prometheus, Satan, and Faust, one of myth's great losers. (Or, in more recent times, winners.) For raising the specter of what has been so poignantly lost (and forgotten), he must be viciously cut down. Civilization has too much riding on its Empire State to give it up.

It is entirely to Fay Wray's credit that at the end, she has an inkling on some level of the nobility of Kong (he is not called King for nothing), and of the tragedy of his fall. At any point in this odyssey Fay Wray could, of course, have gone mad. And she has that option now. I obviously do not think she exercises it. The Kong experience has, let me repeat, consistently destroyed her notions of what the worst could possibly be. Its effect has been to instill the idea that things could always be worse, that the bottom could (is) always open. For most people, the idea of an absolute bottom is necessary; the idea of a continually receding bottom is too great an anxiety. But it may well be the beginning of true wisdom. When Kong finally lies dead (Question: Will—*can*—Kong *ever* die?) on the pavement, it would be easy for Fay Wray to think, "It's over at last," and go about her business. I do not believe that is her thought. If it were, she would still be a very ordinary girl. But she is much more pensive. True, Kong is (seems) dead. It (the nightmare) is (seems) over. But she looks at him more like a lover. Not a lover in flesh any longer: a lover in spirit. Somehow, she senses, Kong's death *is* tragic. And part of its tragic quality is that Kong, in addition to being her lover, has been her teacher—but an unearthly, transcendental, metaphysical teacher. He has exploded her forever out of all possible human complacency, and there at the extreme of anxiety she has found peace, a peace that removes her from the ken of almost all other humans. Kong is dead, but Kong lives in Fay Wray. And if one does not know this, one does not know Fay Wray.

The Examination

Before Fay Wray is offered to Kong, the savages ascertain that she is a virgin and therefore worthy of being offered. This is done by an examination. The examination is conducted by the chief, the elders, and the midwives of the tribe. It is even conceivable that the entire tribe is witness. At any rate, Fay Wray is stripped and laid bare on a (bamboo?) platform in a fire-lit hut. Her legs are forced apart, and black fingers probe, pull, and manipulate her. God only knows what she imagines is going to happen. No doubt she yearns for the good old days on the waterfront. The savages are curious about her in general, and in spite of the business at hand they must be oohing and ahing over peripheral matters like her pale nipples (are they erect?), her skin, and her corn-silk pubic hairs, some of which they pluck (*why?*). Fay Wray has never been so naked, so exposed, so manhandled in her life. Being lower class she has never even had a gynecological examination. She is, in spite of herself of course, phantasmagorically titillated.

Two important things are happening here. The first is that Fay Wray is feeling totally *abandoned* by her world. She could not, at that moment, be further away from it. Nothing in her experience has prepared her for this. Dialogue, for example, is impossible. Imagine, if you will, the total inefficacy of, say, "What are you doing?" or "Please, you're hurting me." Not even females look familiar to her or reachable. Everything is *strange*. Her thoughts, her sensations, are *new*. Needless to say, she also feels existentially abandoned, by her god. Where can God be if there are black fingers in her private parts? This aspect of her experience is to be repeated in the jungle with Kong (during, in effect, their honeymoon) when Kong battles prehistoric creatures (How does one react to real pterodactyls trying to eat one up?). An interesting juxtaposition for her must be the occasion when Kong and her first-mate lover are present and a *Tyrannosaurus rex* attacks. How ineffective and remote must seem the strengths and values of her society then. It is Kong who saves her by killing the lizard.*

The second important function of this episode is that by deranging her from the usual and the known it is preparing her for Kong, a still further derangement. Her despair becomes manageable in part by its *gradual* escalation. Nevertheless, one must see that in the end Fay has been *staggeringly* prepared. It is difficult to say whether Fay knows how much depends on her being a virgin. Had she been an experienced woman, the savages might simply have eaten her outright. In this one respect, her American upbringing has saved her for the greater experience of Kong. As low as she had fallen in America, she had not fallen so low as to sell the precious jewel of herself (eloquent testimony to America's higher standards of living). Poor but pure is an adequate description of the Fay that Carl Denham propositions for Kong.

Fay and Kong's Penis

Fay's attitude toward Kong's penis is a ticklish problem. On the one hand there is the purely bestial part of it (the lesser part, we might say). On the other, there are the several metaphorical tensions. Let us take them in order. Fay, the rather ordinary virgin of the masses, is terrified of Kong's penis, which is huge. No normal girl wants to make love with a giant gorilla. (Yet, how often will a woman describe her lover affectionately as a "big gorilla" or a "hairy ape"?) But Fay, the woman of wisdom through nightmare, is aware that the loss of Kong's penis, although it would probably have killed her

---

*It is interesting, by way of comparison, to note that when Tarzan rescues the prim and proper Jane Porter by killing the concupiscent ape Terkoz, she springs forward, suddenly the primeval woman, and embraces and kisses him with panting lips (*Tarzan of the Apes*, Chapter XIX). Fay has no such reversion.

as it thrilled her, is tragic. It is a loss that will haunt her all her life. She grows from one woman into the other as she sees Kong change from monster supreme to victim supreme. Kong begins as horror and ends as martyr, and in the process his penis is humanized (tenderized). The impossible union between Fay and Kong is symbolic of mankind's fatal *impasse*, the dream of paradise lost irrevocably.* However, this particular symbolic inference is complicated by several other factors, notably the idea that Kong is the black man violating American womanhood and the idea that Kong is the emerging (and rampant) Third World nations. With the first we suffer from colossal penis envy and ego collapse, for we sense Fay's attraction in spite of herself. In the latter, we have violated Kong's sanctuary and brought him back for profit and display, and now he threatens (literally) to screw us. Kong is the classic myth of racist and imperialist represssion and anxiety. Carl Denham is the white entrepreneur *par excellence*. Like Rappaccini in his noxious garden, he fosters evil into being. His manipulation of Fay and Kong for side-show profit and fame is instinctive. He is also stupid. Confronted with tragedy of epic magnitude, he mutters nasally that Beauty killed the Beast. Kong's sex organ (seen, dreamed, inferred, or guessed at) is indicative of our fear of his creative energy. Our destruction of him is confession of our limited imagination. His death will weigh on us more heavily than his life, and it is part of his power that he will be continuously resurrected (by us, in fact).

Fay has come to this knowledge, and it is only in her faith in Kong and his memory that there is any hope for all of us. In these respects, we can say that Kong leaps sexually erect into New York City's streets directly from our nightmares of guilt. We have created him and can no longer awaken from him. Denham is our blundering and loud middleman. And Fay is our vulnerability in a nutshell. Her yielding to Kong, spiritually if not physically, is felt as a betrayal. But a betrayal we ourselves *will*. (We *are* ambivalent

---

*I think that somewhere in the Kong story (I am not sure where) there is a moment (but only a moment) when all *does* seem possible, even Paradise. (Cf. the double vision of America at the end of *The Great Gatsby*.)

about her and Kong.) Hence a frequently suicidal madness that engulfs us. Given time, Fay in her understanding might well have come to love Kong physically, might well have accommodated herself (as the sex books tell us) to Kong's penis. But there is no time. Kong is killed and split into millions of Kongs. And they are coming at us without quarter.

The idea of Kong leading a rat charge on New York City is entirely reasonable. For Americans, rats and cockroaches and bedbugs (vermin) are the living presence of the dark-skinned hordes, the *teeming* masses which spread themselves like crud over the face of the earth. Which is why, of course, the lower we go on the socio-ethno-economic ladder, the less we worry about them (i.e., vermin): they *belong*. A recent eruption of rats on Park Avenue caused matrons to pee in their pants and call the police. The mayor of New York peed in *his* pants when it was discovered that welfare people (epi-vermin) were living in the Waldorf-Astoria (something like finding a rat using your toothbrush). By the same token, our hygienic mode is an attempt to keep America safe (pure). If ever the cockroaches and their brethren get out of hand, the *others* will not be far behind. But spick-and-span as our bathrooms are, we can never lose the awareness of all that dank plumbing in the cellar. Where *do* the pipes (finally) go? What conspiracy is happening down in the sewers? We can never totally lose our anxiety about sitting on the toilet because when the invasion comes, there is where we are vulnerable: a black hand reaching up from the toilet bowl and grabbing our testicles when we are most unprepared. Our behaviorists, meanwhile, allay our fears by telling us all rats can be taught to drink tea. They literally have rats on the brain. Behavioral psychology is the last refuge of the imperialist.

KONG AS TOAD

And now we come to the fairy-tale aspects of the Kong legend. There is, of course, a great deal of charm in the Kong-Fay Wray romance. Consider, for example, the vapidity of Fay Wray before her discovery of Kong. She swallows Denham's tale whole and fantasizes on the purely meretricious glory that will be hers. Any girl with half a brain would have sent Denham packing. But through Kong, Fay Wray becomes a *woman* (*King Kong* is in many ways a *portrait*). She develops a depth of understanding about the nature of life that comes close to being wisdom. Her silences are no longer blank. She is *transformed*, though not at all in the way she first envisioned. We tend to lose sight of this change in her because of all the *noise* (violence) and Kong's dramatic end. But if we concentrate on other aspects of the Kong story, we can begin to see these other possibilities.

For example, his *playfulness*. Even when Kong kills, there is often an element of playfulness in it. He seems more a petulant child than a savage beast. When in the beginning he clutches a writhing Fay Wray in his fist and she is screaming, he cocks his head and looks puzzled, as if to say, "Now what the devil is the matter with this funny little mouse?" When he plucks the screaming woman from her bed and drops her to the street, he is the child who is dropping his toy because it is the wrong one. Even when he is enraged by the sperm bullets the planes shoot at him at the end, he is the child who doesn't understand *why* he is being abused, *why* he is feeling pain. There is more puzzlement than animosity in him.

What I am saying here is that there is a colossal innocence in Kong that exists ostensibly in the the midst of much evil: Kong has no awareness of doing bad things. We must learn to see and understand that. In this respect his inarticulateness is a reinforcement: Kong cannot speak because he is *too young*. But it is even more than that. The words *too young* do not mean, or say, enough. They only shadow, are emblematic. Kong is, in a sense, pre-experience; he is *prior* to experience and the consciousness that it implies. Articulation is the (deceiving) tool of civilization. Further, Kong very often seems on the *edge of articulation*. He seems often about to *tumble* into speech. But he does not. And he does not because he is *imprisoned*. With his arms, especially with his eyes, he reaches out constantly. His eyes are, in fact, the eyes of the lifelong prisoner. They plead, they cry, they scream—but they do not speak.

And the question for us is, first, who is behind those eyes? who is imprisoned within Kong? And second, what is it that will free him? (Perhaps there is a third: *should* he be freed?) The second is, I think, best answered first, because it is very easy to answer. In the familiar story, the princess kisses the frog and he becomes a handsome prince. The kiss I think we may understand to be merely symbolic. In the Kong epic, the kiss would be insignificant. Fay Wray's head would easily fit in Kong's mouth. None of the film's anxieties relate to kissing. No, what is needed to free Kong is for Fay Wray to give herself sexually to Kong out of love and trust. That alone would allow Kong to break through. That she does not do it is part of the tragedy of the story. Although Fay Wray does arrive at a deepness of womanhood at the end, it is a deepness with nowhere to go. She *understands* but now there is no application possible. She is the living memorial of the tragedy of loss. But just what would Kong have been freed into? *Who* is imprisoned within Kong?

That is a difficult question. It is obvious that no mere beast provoked such a depth of response in Fay and others, but rather the *intimations of something other*, within, something frightening, incredible, even transcendent. Otherwise we should not weep for Kong, as we do; his death would not be tragic, as it is. Perhaps Kong is twice or even thrice enchanted, that is, sexual union with Fay would only turn him into a frog, so to speak, leaving her with another ordeal, or several. (Could faith be more severely tried?) For all the change that her encounter with Kong has provoked, Fay has, in one sense, only been *prepared* for the real change, which can come only as the result of one thing. Kong's death leaves her imprisoned as well as him—but with a deep awareness of the change she can now never experience. I don't think that Kong would turn into a handsome prince as a result of union with Fay. Nor do I think that he would turn into, say, a dwarf or a pumpkin, though the ramifications are interesting. Perhaps he would just expire beautifully, or disappear, and it would all be with the seed (so large) he would leave in Fay. Jesus, son of Kong! Or something like. Fay, then, would become the bearer of mankind's redemption. A chance to regain Paradise. For surely Adam in the Garden is *not* so remote from Kong. Would not he, too, have been inarticulate with confusion and rage in the New World? Would not he, too, have been cornered atop the Empire State Building for daring to walk the streets with his penis erect? His affront to civilization would never have been tolerated. Sometimes I think that Kong should be opera. What grand arias Kong would have. But even opera is not *big* enough. Who, in voice, could project the edifice of Kong's gigantic penis? And what a stage would be needed. Alas, in our heads the drama remains. Kong *is* godlike in his unprogenitured existence. That jungle has *always* known Kong. We cannot say Kong, son of. We can only say Kong *is* and Kong *was*. And therein lie much history and sorrow.

Bird-Watching

ONE MORNING THERE WAS A BIRD THAT CALLED IN RHYTHM with my wife's breathing. I had once been a bird-watcher and thought that another time I would have gotten up to look for the bird, for it was indeed a strange call, one I could not identify. But I have let my bird-watching lapse over the years under the pressures of career and domestic life. Still, I listened attentively, for its call kept time perfectly with my wife's early-morning breathing. I thought it was extraordinary, almost as if the bird had some secret connection, as if animals in general had a secret connection, which they rarely displayed, might not even have known, but possessed nevertheless. For a few moments I thought that the bird's call and my wife's breathing were the same, so perfectly were they meshed, that through the vagaries of her respiratory system she was creating the birdlike sound. And, as I say, I listened attentively, preternaturally so. But it was not the same. The two sounds were distinct, one within and one without. I found myself listening, anticipating the call, because I could after all hear my wife's inhalations and exhalations easily. For some reason I imagined the bird as larger rather than smaller, a robin's size rather than a wren's, and as not particularly colorful. Just still and quiet, except for the early morning call and its uncanny attunement, and more or less hidden in deep foliage. And then, after ten or twelve calls, it faded quickly and stopped. I noted that my wife's breathing continued. I also felt impelled to get out of bed to note somehow the occurrence, which awakened my wife. "What time is it?" she said. I made no note, wondered briefly what had happened to my binoculars, and answered, "I don't know." "Isn't the clock going?" she asked. I didn't answer, and she said, "It feels so late." I forebore to mention that to me it felt early because she would have asked why. I didn't know what the bird was, and in fact a bird can call early and late. "Well," she said, "the clock will tell all," and leaned across the bed to see the clock, which was electric. Perhaps, I thought, it wouldn't be plugged in. "It seems to be seven-thirty," she said, "but I don't know whether that's early or late." "Do you know what happened to my binoculars?" I asked. She looked at me a few moments. "I seem to recall that the top came away from the bottom, and then they disappeared anyway. Why are you up so early?" "I heard a bird," I said. "It must have been a loon at least to have awakened you." "We've never heard a loon." "No, but I've read about them. They can be heard for miles. They laugh." "This was somewhat quieter. It was the oddness of it that woke me." She seemed to think about it. "I didn't know we had any odd birds around here. Why don't you come back to bed? It is the weekend, after all." I felt inclined to accept the invitation but didn't move and didn't speak. She picked up a book. "I've got a million things to do today," she said. "Well, you've got the whole day ahead of you." "It'll be gone before I know it. Why don't you track your bird down? Maybe it's something unusual." I sat on the bed and handed her her glasses. "You know, I used to know quite a lot about birds, but it drops away fast." "Well, of course. You have to keep up with things." She set up her pillow and sat up. The quilt dropped away. Her breasts were slightly out of her nightgown. "Maybe you only dreamed about the bird," she said. She was right, of course.

Morsels

IT DOES NOT HAPPEN TO ME OFTEN THAT A REAL MORSEL OF life comes within my reach, so when it does I am not likely to swallow it whole in a moment. Who knows when another would come by? No, rather like a cat with a mouse, I am more likely to tease it, to paw it about, as long as it has a semblance of life, before engulfing it. But one has to be careful. One does not want a moribund or dead thing. What one aims for is that maximum point of possessed life, after which it will cease to be a vital thing. Of course, once one has taken it in, that is not the end of it; there is the slow process of absorption, the sense of *incorporation*, and memory, of course. But these are not the same as the wriggling lifelike thing before one, the thing that just *could* (but won't) escape one. That is a tingling thing; all systems are poised, like a lover, upon it, deliciously anticipating release.

Not everyone understands this about me. I suppose we might warn that one man's meat and drink are not another's. What for one might be a corpse, for me still breathes. On the deepest, truest level I think we might say that the possibilities of human intercourse are contained within this difference, working to keep a live body between the two of us. That, of course, is why society, even family, is so difficult. Loss is unavoidable if we are *both* to remain on the living side of things; and love, thus, is always to a degree tragic, a memory of the never-to-be. When we try to have both, that is, our morsel at its peak, and, say, love also, we usually end up despots, and mutilate souls. Someone must yield sacred territory. But I think, because I understand this so well, that I have succeeded very well indeed in possessing the most possible of both. But I did not always know this. Let me illustrate, however poorly.

In an earlier phase of my life I felt, for a period of time, quite homeless. It was one of those domestic things that crop up even in the best-regulated lives. I fell in with a younger group, on the fringes of art. They were an unhealthy-looking bunch, but unambitious and vastly tolerant. It was their custom most evenings to gather in one or another of their drab establishments and watch old movies while smoking and nodding away. They did not seem to go in much for sex, or eating, or talking. They seemed to drift from one day into the next, carrying along without fuss any flotsam, like myself, caught in their desultory current. I admired their ability to be with the moment, and their indifference to anything without, or to the next day. It was enough for them to be together, warm, resting, looking, smoking, and drifting in the near dark. We were like snug happy hedgehogs in the dead of winter.

The first few times I was unsure of my welcome and remained inconspicuous. It is true I was *with* them, but not, as they say, *of* them; I did not feel comfortable. I had no idea what went on in their heads, nor what I might gain from them. It was all very amorphous. The movies seemed invariably bad, and the worse they were, the better it seemed they liked them. They drowsed a lot, and at moments, always unaccountably to me, they laughed like hyenas or made jokes I never got. I gathered they had seen the films before because they could quote from them. Then, also, they were young, as I said. That makes for a difference. They also smelled a little, but it was more a communal than an unpleasant smell. It made me feel all the more tangibly with them. We created our own atmosphere, like a dewy web, and at that time in my life I savored it and wanted to make the most of it, and to express my gratitude.

Accordingly, one night a week or so later, feeling an abundance of sanctuary, I said suddenly, "This is just great, absolutely great! Fantastic!" I could perceive they were startled. It was as if someone had turned on a bright light. They shifted positions, opened eyes, looked, blinked, then began, like ruffled cats, to ease down again, absorbing quickly. But I could not stop. I went on about the homeyness of it all, the beautiful ageless egalitarianism, and so on. They got up after a while, stretched, put on a few dim lights, and began talking, shifting on their feet. I felt I had finally become one of them. And no sooner did I feel that than I noticed the group was steadily dwindling until I was left alone with my presumed host. "Well, an early night," I said. He smiled vaguely. I bade him good night. There was no question apparently of the two of us watching a movie. I had a sneaking feeling they had all been sucked into another room, or another apartment, and were already curled up to the hissing noises of radiators, watching another in their unending series of forgotten movies. While I, instead, found myself walking empty streets on a cold February night.

I found a diner at one point and had coffee. Everyone there (and there were six of us) looked similarly thrust out. I say thrust out because it dawned on me that I had been egregrious in some way. I had fiddled too much with my morsel. But I did not then have the same powers of reflection I have now. I felt rather woebegone, and that night, one of the coldest of my life, was the beginning of my return to the regular paths of life, however unsatisfactory. I do feel, however, that over the years I have learned, and learned better. I have, for example, a good friend who speaks too loudly at museums, probably because he is a physicist. He feels that looking is not enough; things must be explained. He also is not content to keep a parallel path when talking to you in the street but must lean in on you until you are in the gutter. He wants you not only to hear him but to be engulfed by him. I understand his awkwardness but have told him nothing, for he is an original in his way. Nor do I particularly avoid him, though he is getting to be a nuisance. No, I practice tolerance, even to the point of obtuseness. In that sense, I have truly gone beyond my young friends. I am keeping *him* from the cold. And I suppose one might say *I* am pawing him about a bit, but not, at least not yet, too much. He is still a live morsel.

Walking

IT IS IMPOSSIBLE TO WALK WITH MY WIFE. OUR SPEEDS AND our metaphysics are in conflict. Her goal is to cover ground, mine to see. And naturally the more I see, the slower I walk; and the slower I walk, the more I see. My walk sometimes cannot exceed a few dozen feet; her walk sometimes covers miles. So here I stand, looking at infinite small things, and there she stands, far away on a hill top, not seeing me except as a speck in nature's vast composition. When we compare notes, it is to translate from one language into another. It is not that I object to walking long distances. On several occasions I have walked five or more miles, particularly on beaches, though I have also taken hours to cover several hundred yards. It could be anything that arrests me, a bird call, a leaf, the rocks, the feel of slow, almost non-, movement. Nor do I claim any superiority to my style of walking. My wife, I am sure, sees things that I do not, and more of the things that I do see. Still we cannot get together on this. I cannot sustain the urge to cover distance. This is my objection to cars, trains, and planes. That is why I love so much Thoreau's remarks that he had traveled a good deal in Concord and that the best way to get to Boston was on foot. I imagine he took his whole life to get to Boston, and never quite made it. It would surely have killed him if he had. So my wife and I walk, and we very soon reach that point of conflict where I am dallying too much. If I speed up, I feel that I am missing too much. If she slows down, she becomes restless and bored. She is then very likely to lie down and go to sleep, after which she is ready to cover ground, having indulged me. But although I then usually walk long distances with her, it is not true that she has indulged me. I let it go. It is important, but not important to belabor, for the difference is fundamental. A recent incident will indicate how fundamental. We had begun our walk and passed our metaphysical point of no return. I saw her stretched out a mile or so before me as I puttered forward. For over an hour she was out of sight. Then I saw her returning. And finally we were together again. Her face was flushed with the exercise, she seemed bouyant and energized, much in contrast to my quiet, rather somber demeanor. "Well," she said, "and did you have an exciting walk?" The irony was not lost on me. "Yes," I answered, "did you?" "It was *beautiful*," she said. I offered no further comment, and I could see that she was annoyed. It was one thing not to walk, and bad enough, but then the least I could do was to have something to say about my time or to ask about hers. Finally, she burst out, "Well, what did you *do*?" I looked at her a few seconds, then answered, "I died a little." At first she was confused, then angry. She took it as some kind of accusation, though I had not intended it as such. It was the truest comment I could make at the time. Her consternation seemed about to explode into chaos, so I laughed. "It's all right," I said. "It happens all the time." "That's a hell of a thing to say," she answered. "It's stupid. It's sick." And she began walking again. Neither of us spoke. In fact, we never mentioned the exchange again. Perhaps she was right. Perhaps it was sick of me. Nevertheless, each time we walk, I do die a little.

Fox-Trot and Other Matters

IT IS KNOWN OF THE GREAT RUSSIAN ARTIST LIUBOV POPOVA that she loved to dance the fox-trot. I know this to be so because I read it recently in a learned journal. Yet it is a fact rarely mentioned in scholarly works about her times or catalogs on her art. Instead, what is emphasized is her revolutionary fervor, her anticipation of later developments in art, her subsequent suppression and sad end. So, too, of her fellow artists—Rodchenko, for example, Tatlin, Lunarcharsky, Filanov; despair, concentration camps, bitterness, ostracism, slander—who knows what exactly? It is all very sad. The passion for a glorious future wiped out. And so it was an unexpected delight, a positive relief, to learn that Popova loved the fox-trot. It is an entire history and biography in itself. The words could easily be carved in stone. How quaint it seems now, in this age of body frenzy, to think of her passion. How simple and decent, although no doubt there were some who thought her brazen. Is it possible that amongst her fellow artists there was one who loved dogs, another who gave flowers to strange women on impulse, and still another who was inordinately proud of his boots? Very likely. For is it not true of most, if not all, of us? We have these insignificant little qualities. And how wonderfully humanizing it is to be made aware of it, especially in the thick of history, so to speak. I am thinking right now of the man, a soldier, an officer, who gave lollipops to the children as they walked into the gas chamber. How characteristic a gesture, precisely what is lost in an account of his youth in Heidelberg, his medals, his years of service, his patriotism. Without the fox-trot and the lollipop we do not adequately know our subject. Of course it is not always charming. How much is? And unless we squint we might not even see it. Our children, for example, do the most interesting things when they feel we are not looking. Sometimes they shock us. A learned French critic and philosopher has gone so far as to say that truth is more likely at the edge of things than at the center, that it is as likely to be tossed off in a sneeze, we might say, as in some public grandiloquence. And so I return to Popova; Liubov. What did she wear when she danced the fox-trot? Was she pretty? Did the men watch her closely? In the sad days that came for all of them later, did she remember the music, her swaying body? Could she still smile? Did the officer remember the grateful eyes of naked children? Did he think of lollies when he died? Perhaps he went to a special lolly heaven, where all the lollies had grateful eyes and swayed thinly for eternity. Somewhere I think Popova must be dancing her fox-trot. I have seen her circles and angles and machinery, all hard edges and testimony to her faith in a rational and technological future. Sentiment was not for her. She might even have worn comradely boots when she danced. Who knows? But the steps she took made them light as ballerina slippers. The little children suck their lollipops. Popova floats. Time moves on. And we must close our eyes to slits, look sideways without seeming to, and remember all; all.

Firm Ground

PERHAPS THE FIRST SIGN OF OFFICER X'S AMBIVALENCE WAS his inability to make his face conform to his duties. It was a handsome face, just slightly on the pretty side but compensated for by the severity of his haircut and a gashlike mustache. When he first came as a replacement, we were terrified. We had adapted ourselves to the pattern of his predecessor and now, like old wives remarried, felt a mad anxiety to learn the new one. But he was impossible. His smiles and frowns, his ennui, his excitement bore no resemblance to anything we knew. He had no tics, no special mannerisms that we could read; we were unable to fathom the motives of his actions. Our experience seemed all for nothing. For weeks we prepared ourselves for the worst. We were certain he was an absolute scheming devil and we would be wiped out when we least expected or deserved it. We exhausted all our reserves with worry and made ourselves vulnerable in a thousand ways. Then, quite suddenly, perhaps because our backs were nearly broken, everything changed. It was given us to know that he was no super-trickster, but merely a man ignorant of his role and therefore uncomfortable and awkward. It was an enormous relief. Strength surged back into our bodies. Our thoughts rioted with hope. We had sly invisible smiles for one another. For once the wrong man had been chosen. The world was reborn for us.

For several months we mutely lavished our sympathy on him. We understood profoundly the impossibility, the outrage, of his position. We endured almost lovingly his odd hesitations, his aborted movements, his tonal blunders. We would have slapped his back had it been allowed. And we suffered for him when his subordinates gave him queer looks. When he ordered some of us sent to the hospital or killed for obvious infractions we excused him. We even condemned and executed them before he did, and suffered pangs of anxiety over his slowness. And, of course, we waited. We waited for some overt sign, however small, that he knew about us, that he cared, that in some infinitesimal way he would look out for us. We watched him intensely. He became our private study. He brutalized our feeble capacity for wonder. We brooded on every wrinkle of his clothing, were alert as dogs to every nuance of sound, stood breathless to force some significant act upon the stillness. What we wanted was not merely an idle gesture of reprieve, some moment of kindness or warmth tossed off in madness, but a deliberate act. We wanted it to be conscious, naked, a pinpoint beam of light of the intensest magnitude, striking into the darkness of our hearts. Several times he nearly fooled us. Once a man ill with dysentery was being beaten, and he shot him through the head. We judged it a merciful act, for the man could never have survived both the dysentery and the beating. Our hopes leapt like hungry flames. But in the end we denied him. It was too gross to pass our barriers. We decided that the man's noise had upset him, that he was uncertain of the situation's decorum. He had merely acted awkwardly. And so it went.

It was not very long before we were furious with him. He tried our patience. He abused our meager souls. One sign was not too much to ask. We humiliated him in our fantasies. He was impotent, homosexual, a mama's boy. We joked about his baby fat, the size of his penis, the sordid things he made his subordinates do for him. He had let us down. He had closed off the horizon, made infinite once again the boundaries of our enclosure. And we cried, alone before our sleep, at our horrible expenditure. But at the back of our minds, we left him a last chance. This we never admitted. It was a private crazy thing. It kept us alive.

And then he resolved everything for us. It was a man named Rubin. He had been in the camp two years and had the cunning of a rat. He conserved himself at every point. He sucked strength out of every spare second. He ravaged even the smells of cooking bodies for nourishment. He learned to feel death in the air and disappear. He was bland and inconspicuous to an extreme, but wiry with the purpose of life, survival. We hated, feared, and envied Rubin. He had no friends.

It was the first formation of the day, and Officer X, smelling of cologne, picked Rubin out blindly and asked why he was missing buttons. Rubin was terrified, though only we knew it. All the gods he had carefully cultivated had desrted him utterly. The plain fact was that everyone had missing buttons. They had long since been stolen or lost. Rubin began to mutter something, but he was slapped across the face. He turned white and stood there silently, calling on reserves of cunning that would always be unequal to the situation before him. Officer X found the resolution to laugh suddenly. He turned to his subordinates, whereupon they laughed also. In a high-pitched, shrill, ecstatic voice he demanded again of Rubin where were his buttons. Before Rubin could answer, he was kicked in the testicles. As he sank to his knees, still silent, Officer X kicked him full in the mouth. We saw the teeth break and lie in his mouth. And then, after what seemed a long time, the blood, a sudden huge bubble of it, as if Rubin had held on to it as long as he could. Behind impassive faces we reviewed Rubin's dilemma. Should he endure all the punishment in silence because at the end of it he would still be allowed to live, if he could? Or was it to go all the way, and should he therefore beg or perhaps even make some impotent gesture of defiance, retrieve some remote memory of self, of dignity, before he died? We felt all the despair of his loss, the thousands of meaningless calculations in Rubin's career, his infinite tinkerings with fate. We were too numb for nausea; Rubin was more than personal. He looked up at Officer X and uttered what we would never have believed possible. It was more horrible than any dying shriek. He had made a last desperate calculation and was betting everything. Choking with his blood he said, "I, too, was once a lover of beauty!" Officer X kicked him in the head and he fell over dead. He had lost.

Rubin's death paralyzed us. But it also relieved us. One of us, insane with confusion and hopelessness, rushed forward and kicked Rubin's body. For this he got his head smashed in with a rifle butt. We did not mind. It was a small price to pay for getting back on firm ground.

Teddy and I Go Kong

IT HAS BEEN MONTHS SINCE TEDDY AND I HAVE BEEN HOME. Sometimes it seems like years, but I know it has only been months because here and there I get intimations of real time and space. Teddy is my infant son. He was just born, but already he is aging rapidly. In the beginning he was all flippers and stumps, but then things began to grow out. I thought, for a time, he would be octoploid, but I was wrong. After the fourth month he settled down nicely. He loved his nursing but gave it up early, in fact after his seventh week. I took him, on that occasion, to see *King Kong*. It was a hit with him from the start. He cooed and gurgled throughout the movie. And we have since seen it a dozen times or more. Soon he will be a match for Kong, but of that later. It started out as a perfectly ordinary occasion. That is, Teddy was dressed especially for the occasion by his mother. He wore a blue sailor suit. I was given a diaper change and a bottle. In the theater I bought popcorn and thoroughly enjoyed it. Between the first and second showing of *Kong* I washed it down with orange soda. Between the second and third showing, I urinated. There was no fourth showing, but the theater remained dark, and Teddy and I slept like babies.

That night the paraplegics in W-4 held a strategy meeting. They were playing the C.P. basketball team the following night and, although they had only three good limbs among them compared to a full count for the C.P.'s, the C.P.'s were all violent shakers and could not call their plays fast enough. It was, as expected, a slaughter, the paraplegics winning 2-0. Four broken wheelchairs and some mangled mechanical limbs, but that was a matter for Properties.

The next day we went down to Times Square, had a quick orange drink and donut, and made the 10:00 a.m. movie. It was an early Wayne war movie, and the Japs fell like flies. I offered Teddy his bottle, but he knocked it out of my hand. "Corn," he said, meaning popcorn. I immediately gave him some. He had never spoken before. Overnight he seemed to have grown. I thought about calling his mother, but the day was still young. The second time through the war movie I felt I was having double vision. And then I realized what it was. The Japs seemed to be Viet-Cong. In the paraplegic preview the Puerto Rican attendants turned into Cong fighters every night. W-4 became a battlefield, they infiltrated, and mutilated the men even more, cutting digits of fingers, ears, cocks. Those men were really screaming in terror. But during the day the P.R. attendants were very nice, especially about masturbation and things. And never took money. Only occasionally did they seem to be plotting in a foreign language.

By and large the C.P.'s were a dirty bunch, pooping and peeing in their pants when excited. Their cheerleaders never finished one cheer the entire evening. Corporal Puglisi, who had no legs, but one good arm, was top scorer, making the one basket (a three-footer) of the game. He also played dirty, punching the C.P.'s whenever he could since by the time they finished protesting, no one could remember the details. It was during the game that Puglisi got his idea for the annual pageant. Something about the way the paraplegic team rolled down the court ("in stately majesty," he said) made him think they should do "Victory at Sea."

Teddy meanwhile had fallen asleep. When he awoke, Wayne was mopping up again, and we left. We went next door and stayed a week. They were doing a Judy Canova festival, and Teddy learned to eat hot dogs and sing "I Didn't Know the Gun Was Loaded," a real Canova hit. He kept clenching his fist and I recognized it as a Kong trait. He was getting very big. As we worked our way down 42nd Street, the movies got raunchier. I wasn't sure I liked exposing Teddy, but he seemed to take it all in his stride. Sometimes he simply misunderstood. Installment eight of fifteen on *The Sensuous Man* was on tongue movements. All the men in the audience had their tongues out and were exercising by the numbers as per instruction. Teddy went right along with them, cooing and gurgling with delight. He clutched my arm throughout, and only later did I discover the black and blue marks.

"Victory at Sea" was a flop. It consisted mainly of a tableau that became a slowly moving flotilla on wheels, with Puglisi as admiral. It only dawned gradually on the select audience of concerned citizens that the flotilla was bearing down on *them*, but they had nowhere to go. Puglisi's secret orders were a stump for every guest, and he damn near succeeded. Everyone took the upset well. Polite smiles and titters. Raquel Raquel, popularly known as the bazoom queen, retrieved the situation with a rousing song, the first two stanzas of which went:

> Kill a Jap, kill a Cong
> With a bong, bong, bong,
> And we'll all take vict'ry
> In our stride!
> Thrill the boys, Jews or goys,
> Never say, "Oi, oi, oi,"
> We're the vets, place your bets,
> We have pride!

She was followed, after an encore (*Bullets or Bums*), by Gerald Panucci, a new Borsht comic, who told some really swell jokes like where does a quadraplegic get the ring when he marries? (And what happens when he gets a hard-on?) He felt it was better every time to take the bull by the horns and call a spade a spade. Ice cream and cake topped off the event, and it was all early to bed after a full day.

The more we saw *King Kong* the more we seemed to see in it. We, of course, went right to the heart of the matter in our wonder-ment—namely what would sexual union be like between Kong and the maiden? That is what throbbed behind every viewer's mind. And that is why those men raced through the jungle with such urgency. They must get to her before Kong has an erection and penetration takes place. Yet repeated viewings reveal Kong to be a perfect gentleman in that respect. Or was it simply that he could not find it? Or having found it, believe it was what it seemed to be? (*What?*) Beast that he was, he revealed the civilized man's flaw of too much thought and insufficient instinct. Had he settled down to quick domesticity, there would have been no frenzy. (No one can think for a moment that anyone would have wanted to save the maiden after she had been *used*. Like all women, the blond (?) beauty needed only a good consummation, and in time his finer qualities would have been apparent to her. In that tropical, magical, pre-Edenic jungle there might well have been little Konglets to while away the years, and a new legend for mankind. But it was not to be. Kong could not find it, or didn't know what it was. (*It?*) In this frustration, this loss, this dream movie rises to tragic heights. (Puzzling fact: Where *is* Kong's penis? It is never shown, yet he is only a big ape. What offense in having him approach the girl initially with an erection?—to give point to her screams.) (Question: Is Kong *female*? Is this a disguised lesbian movie, with Kong really a butch Queen Kong?)

Meanwhile, in W-4 it's quiet time. Medal of Honor winner and Paraplegic of the Year, Harold Rosenbloom, is visiting the men. It is official and it's a morale booster. Mainly because Harold has left W-4 and entered into the mainstream of American life. Married to an orthodox girl from Yemen (a former street cleaner in Tel Aviv), he has adopted half a dozen black orphans from the ghetto and had them circumcised. There will be no authentic, genital Rosenblooms because Harold, in the process of killing 78 *gooks* from three months to 91 years of age, has lost *all* appendages. He is a true quintiplegic. (The rumor is that his wife blows his nose, as is only right.) He is also incapable of any gainful employment because he is stupid. However, he tells the men that, in addition to his total-plus disability, he makes $14,000 to $20,000 a year, not including expenses, speaking to paraplegic and community groups in the Northeast area. (Suburban housewives, he confided, get excited by stumps, anything stiff, steady, and ready, ha-ha.) Harold gets anything he wants because he gave for his country. No politician in his district would dare to run for office without having his picture taken shaking Harold's shoulder. Harold will be rich (he even endorses products) one day for he is a pioneer in a new career-field. Puglisi throws the only fly in the ointment. "What happens," he wants to know, "when we all get into the act and there ain't enough amputees to go around?" Rosenbloom replies that he has never considered himself an "amputee." Puglisi has to satisfy himself with that for an answer. But later Rosenbloom says that with 2,000-3,000 new paraplegics being produced a year, not to mention the fact of expanded wars, new wars, and secret wars (and the increasing domestic paraplegics), there is room for more like him. There is every reason to believe, he says, that more than half of them will be in permanent institution-type situations, thus providing a continuing circuit for morale-boosters like himself. None of it makes much sense, but Puglisi grunts and appears to be thinking about it. In honor of the occasion, the men have prepared a special demonstration that Harold will be sure to appreciate. Government research has just come up with its first hygiene unit for war heroes. Clarence Johnson, a black boy from Newark, demonstrates. It is a cross between a dental and electric chair, and Clarence is quite excited. The P.R. aides get him hooked up in about five minutes. Then Clarence, who has no arms, but all the control of the natural ex-athlete, gets to work with his feet and shoulders. After ten minutes he is a mass of sweat, but everyone is rooting for him. For a few seconds it looks as if everything will go kaput, but in a burst of concentration he comes through, he succeeds, he wipes his own ass for the first time in two years. There is a lot of the sound of one hand or foot clapping.* Obviously it is not as good yet as a Yemenite special, and Rosenbloom leaves quickly, which is rather rude of him. Next year the men are promised a total environment machine to handle toothbrushing, light washing, combing, scratching, even sex. The men argue a lot over who will be the first to live in it.

Teddy has positively bloomed. He now eats, in addition to Hershey Bars, hot dogs, donuts, popcorn, Baby Ruths, Mounds, Almond Joy, twizzlers of all flavors, pizza, hamburgers, knishes,

---

*Clarence will be a frequent source of pleasure and amusement as the movie progresses. For example, on one occasion right after the machine wipes his ass it smears his face. "Let them eat shit!" he shouts with a shit-eating grin. He is used to setbacks.

Bit-O-Honey, O'Henry, Non Pareils, and chocolate kisses, which he unwraps himself and eats with kissing sounds. Although he still must crawl to the bathroom, he is toilet-trained. He is growing hair in his arm pits, and elsewhere, too, I suspect. I called his mother the other day and we had a pleasant conversation.

"Where are you?" she said.

"At the movies," I answered.

"Oh," she said.

And hung up. We have always lived in New York City and enjoyed it. The only thing I don't like about Teddy's going to the bathroom alone is that they are so dirty. He comes back wet and stinking from the urine on the floor. Fortunately I have the extra diaper, which has become a rag of all purposes. My wife is from Connecticut, originally, and our first joke was my pronouncing her home state "Conneckticut." The bottle I have lost. Teddy never needed it. Some rat probably sucked all the milk away while we were sleeping. Last night I had the bizarre dream that I was Kong and my wife was the white maiden. Teddy, of course, was our first-born. It is unbelievable how large he is getting. Even though he can only kneel at the urinal, he gets everything in quite easily. It is possible that we are being followed. Or observed. I regret that movies these days do not have the *March of Time* or *Movie-Tone News*. I'm not up on things.

The paraplegics in W-4 are kept regularly posted, of course. They have a great interest in the wars because part of them, they feel, is still there. It is a psychic thing. Fortunately they have their diversions. Their head nurse, Hewlitt, for example, is gorgeous. She has ripe round buttocks, milk bursting breasts with large nipples, a small but strong waist, and zooming hips that make pleasant handful bulges where they meet her thighs. If you put your hand in the dark corner of her thighs and body, it is flesh like warm water, smooth and sinkable. But apparently no cunt. At least that is the word. Another diversion is TV. The food is terrible, but the men play games. Monopoly is very popular. All the sex magazines, of course. Jane Fonda, minus a leg, hangs on the wall. And Marilyn Monroe with a double mastectomy. Under Marilyn's picture: "War is hell." Raquel Raquel hangs with hooks covering her pubic hair demurely. The staff encourages these interests. They find it realistic. Some day these men will want to marry legless, even cuntless, girls and settle down somewhere. Perhaps that is why Hewlitt is head nurse. And who plays head night nurse? That is a very interesting question.

We saw Kong for the fifteenth time about six months later. The fact is, my wife is very hairy. She has hair all over her body and shaves it several times a day. What is quite clear but has never been commented on is that Denham, the impresario of the movie, is really a mad scientist in the tradition of Nathaniel Hawthorne's heroes. When he says "Beauty and the Beast," he has only one thought in mind, namely an unholy copulation. For this he needs, and finds, a dumb blond (I insist on that). He is also, obviously, a voyeur, because he intends to *watch*. Can you imagine that scene?— *King Kong laying Fay Wray*. Denham can, and it is surely a knock-out. It occurs to me now that the movie does show Kong's penis, at the very end, when he is climbing it to escape. When the planes come and shoot their tiny sperm bullets, it is not so much at Kong as at his penis, to the tip of which he has finally got Fay Wray. And when he lets go of it, he falls to his death. The penis is kept as a monument, hollowed out with offices and elevators, and called the Empire State Building. And New York is called the Empire State (the King Kong penis state: it is our answer to the jungle out of which Kong came). What must that do to the psyches of New Yorkers? But some of them know that it is really Kong's penis, still living among us, and steer clear of it. So Denham is a *voyeur*. He is also, among other things, a demon hymenologist. His alter ego is the black chieftain or witch doctor who says to Fay Wray in his guttural best, "You go to Kong!" I don't really mind my wife's hair, but it does raise certain doubts at times. Teddy accidentally strangled a man in the crook of his arm today. It was a drunk who had fallen asleep on his shoulder. In a week his body will smell and they will take him out. But we shall have moved on.

In the interests of normalcy, Dr. Prothero (Eddie Prothero, to his friends), a guidance counselor, used to bring his plump wife and children to visit W-4 often. "Let 'em see a little normal, everyday nookie," he used to say to the staff. His wife giggled a lot and took a great deal of poking until one day a hook got caught and ripped her dress off. In ten seconds, thanks to other hooks, she was a shivering, giggling, weeping, naked mass, and Dr. Eddie never brought her again. He thought hooks in his wife's cunt and up her ass was going too far. It was not normal. No woman ever got pregnant with a hook up her ass.

That is not Kong's problem. His problem is that he has to come all the way to New York City to find his penis. Meanwhile he has to sublimate a lot by fighting pterodactyls and lizards. He must be a little confused because he has carried a woman across the threshold and now what does he do? (Incidentally, what did he do with all the black maidens he had been receiving each year from the natives? The answer, I think, is obvious, although not mentioned in the film. He ate them. Those black maidens never really knew what they were screaming about. They must have been quite surprised when he put them in his mouth. He might not even have been hungry, but what else could he do? However, for Fay Wray it is different. King Kong never knew true love until Fay Wray. She is his destiny. He knows, on some deep instinctive level, that she is not to be eaten, that her use is something other. With Fay Wray something is born in Kong, and reborn in the world. And so he must go to New York City to claim his penis.) It is odd, in a way, that New York City should have Kong's penis. There is a guilt about it, but buried. And Kong, in the jungle, has a sense of incompleteness. (There is never even a hint of a Mrs. Kong.) Although he is big, and a great fighter, there is something of the child in him. It shows, for example, when he holds Fay Wray in his fist (she is screaming) and he cocks his head quizzically at her. There is a certain charm and innocence that is not repeated until the end when the sperm bullets are hurting him and all he is doing is holding on to his penis with one hand and Fay Wray with the other. (Where is his mama?) What is this squealing doll and what does she want from me? He has no awareness yet, but it will come to him. He will have to go through hell first, and when he finds what he needs, what he lacks, it will be too late. For Kong must be destroyed before he finds his penis, gains complete possession of it. Once he regains it, there will be no stopping him. Fay Wray will have had it. At this perception we can see that Carl Denham is also either God or Satan or a gypsy fortune teller. Obviously Kong will never be a solid citizen. He will want only to screw Fay Wray. For that is his destiny and Denham knows it. But he is a business man also, so he wants to film it, then stage it. And perhaps that is his mistake. He is so busy filming and staging that he doesn't realize it is *happening*. Beauty has captured the Beast. Now it is the Beast's turn to capture Beauty. And that will be history.

(A small digression here. There is a wonderful scene where Kong, in search of Fay, is climbing up the side of a building. A middle-aged woman is sleeping alone in a room. Perhaps it is her first visit to the big city. Something, perhaps instinct, awakens her, and she sees Kong's eye looking at her. It takes up almost the whole window. Of course she screams her head off, which only makes Kong more curious. Is this possibly Fay? He reaches in and gropes with his hand as the woman continues screaming and tries to avoid the hand, but she cannot. Kong scoops her up, takes her outside the window, realizes she is not Fay, and crushes and/or drops her to her death. This is what you might call a nightmare come true. The folks back home were right. But it could have been worse.)

The big push in W-4 comes on a Tuesday night. Puglisi loses two fingers of his last limb to the P.R.-Cong invaders. He is sore as hell about it but doesn't lose his captaincy of the basketball team. The Cong are small and come through the air vents about 2:00 a.m. with foliage in their helmets. They speak Spanish and carry razor sharp machetes to make the men think they are Cuban cane-cutters. But they don't fool anybody. They are Viet-Cong, and they are taking over the city. Right now they are living by the thousands in the sewers. At night they come up like rats and waterbugs, infiltrating the weak links in the chain of civilization. Of course they smell, particularly of hair oil and garlic. A strange thing about them is that if you sleep you don't notice them because they leave you alone. Even if you are awake but *pretend* to be asleep you can usually escape mutilation. Their main intent is just to pass through.

51

After that, who knows where they go? Perhaps they raid the kitchen. Anyway, Puglisi is stupid. He is obviously awake and stares at them. They lop off two fingers, and he says, "Hey, what the fuck—" and is silent. Probably he is in a state of shock at seeing the blood spurt. But the Cong never forget they are P.R. attendants either. They give him an injection, stop the bleeding, and bandage him. Puglisi then sleeps like a baby. Later, the next day, he will agonize and rant and rave about what the FBI and CIA are and are not doing. The country, he says, is going to the dogs. No one is inclined to disagree.

Meanwhile, Teddy and I have been seeing some Ronald Reagan and Ronald Coleman movies. (It is a Ronnie month.) Reagan loses a leg or two in one, but it is all very odd. Odd because Kong is somehow getting into their movies. At first he was just a shadow vaguely showing through the screen. It seemed he was there, in the theater, standing behind the screen, looking out at us, maybe waiting. It was a very scary thing. And then, suddenly, he's *in* the movie. Ronald Coleman is making love like a true Englishman. "My dear," he says, rolling the "r," "you are simply adorable tonight, ravishing, in fact. Quite." And as he is smiling at the woman, Kong's right arm comes from off screen, his hand grabs Coleman's neck and squeezes. Coleman turns white. It is clear he wants to say something off-handed and polite to cover the fact that he is being strangled. But he doesn't. He can't. He flaps a little, shrugs, and collapses. Then Kong's arm withdraws. The woman shakes Coleman. "Darling," she says (she is ad-libbing desperately), "darling, are you all right?" He obviously isn't any more, and she screams. And that, of course is what Kong is waiting for. Maybe this screamer is Fay Wray. But it is also the end of the movie. It's been changed completely. In another movie, Robert Taylor is a buffalo hunter. He is killing all the buffalo. He is not eating them. At one point he is chasing a herd of buffalo. Suddenly, they turn and chase *him*. And they are being led by Kong. Taylor is frightened. He whips his horse and croaks out harsh commands. But Kong and the buffalos are gaining. It looks pretty weird, Kong leading all those buffalos, but also sort of majestic. Soon Kong's hands are almost on the back part of Taylor's horse. The moment is very tense. The horse, of course, is terrified. He has never had a giant gorilla leading a buffalo charge at him. What is going through his head is impossible to describe. And then, quite suddenly and unexpectedly—*Teddy* lets out a blood-curdling roar that makes half the audience pee in their pants. My hair stands on end. He is becoming monstrous. I could never explain to his mother. Thank god he still recognizes me.

Saluting the flag is always a problem in W-4. Every morning the loudspeaker emits the national anthem and the pledge. Then some news flashes of interest to the men, and stock quotations, followed by restful music. Raquel Raquel has gotten married for the third time. The lucky man is her body guard. It will make for a good working arrangement. On the J. Carson show, Raquel reveals that she wears only pajama bottoms to bed—"To let my nipples breathe," she says. It drives the audience wild. "And what about your cunt?" screams Puglisi. They turn off the TV, and so to bed. Which is not so peaceful as it sounds. The rats have found W-4 a haven. First of all, administration and personnel deny that there *are* rats. Then, the men have limited mobility against them. Third, food is plentiful, or rather garbage, which is not swept up or collected daily. Most of W-4 sleep with tubes on their penises. The tubes lead to containers on the floor which should be emptied regularly but are not. The rats lick the overflow (probably for the residual drug content). Sometimes they knock the containers over and drink directly from the tube, like babies. Conrad, who has all his limbs but is helpless from the neck down because of a spinal injury, is slowly getting his fingers chewed off because he has no sensation there. It took him a year to learn to breathe properly again. One night he woke up, saw a rat gnawing on his thumb, thought he was dreaming, and went back to sleep again. It is only a matter of time before the rats get into bed with him. But he is very philosophical about it. He has severe burns over much of his body because an attendant left him in a defective shower a month ago. He looked like a boiled lobster but felt nothing. The smell of putrescent flesh is giving the other men some relief from the rats. To help Conrad out, they throw their garbage under his bed to divert the rats from his body. Conrad wishes he could get a hard-on and talks a lot about Raquel Raquel. The men humor him. He cannot even feel himself defecating. Lately he has given up his crew cut for a hippie-style hairdo. Conrad was a marine at eighteen and got hit by rocket fire at nineteen. His family objects strenuously to his hair, and the latest word is that they will not visit him until he cuts it. They don't want the neighbors smirking and saying, "We hear Conrad's gone hippie." Conrad has given several of the rats names and thinks he can distinguish their sexes. If he survives he wants to be either a radio announcer or a folk singer.

I can just imagine Kong leading a rat charge. On New York City. "Flash: thirty million rats, lead by the notorious Kong, have just demolished Perth Amboy, and are heading for the Hudson Tunnel. It is estimated that by the time they reach the Tunnel their ranks will have swollen to fifty million." Wouldn't that set New York City on its heels? And if they were organized—ten million over the George Washington Bridge, ten million through the Lincoln Tunnel, ten million scouring through Westchester, and so on— what a movie it would make. They would leave one exit open, say the Brooklyn-Battery Tunnel. But the people in Brooklyn would have only that same single exit. Picture it. A million Manhattanites surging in at one end and a million Brooklynites at the other. They meet in the middle, scream at each other to turn back, and get mashed against one another by the frenzied masses behind them. By the time the people at either end get the idea that the tunnel's impassable, it is filled like a gigantic strudel, a rat strudel. What a job to clean it out. I told Teddy about it and he nearly bit off my arm. He was very excited. I remind him that I am his father and he calms down. People definitely stay clear of us now in the movies. We've seen Garbo, Stanwyck, Bogart, all of them. I don't feed Teddy any more, although he is growing all the time. He does not seem to be hungry. I suspect that he considers people lollipops, but I have no evidence as yet. Next week we see the Weissmuller Tarzan movies, and I am apprehensive. I think spring is approaching.

Even in W-4 the seasons change. Rat babies everywhere.

Raquel Raquel has annulled her marriage because of physical cruelty. Puglisi spins out theories endlessly. Conrad has dictated a proposal of marriage to her. The men are considering challenging the multiple sclerotics to a track meet. Hewlitt has admitted to a cunt. And the Cong have suspended night raids to celebrate Easter. The first Cambodian paraplegics have arrived, and it is a diversion to watch them adjust to limbless life or lifeless limbs. The ward has adopted a war orphan, Chang-Wu, a bright-eyed and alert Vietnamese who has a pet water buffalo he thinks is his mother. The secret aim is to get Chang-Wu to the U.S. so he can masturbate all of them in payment for their sacrifices. The new men don't find this funny. The Anti-Defamation League is sending a speaker next week, also the Catholic War Veteran's League. The movie very much has an on-going sense of life, and I am getting inklings of how it will all come out.

Kong is magnificent. He is *Civilization and Its Discontents* in a nutshell. Kong is dead! Long live Kong! Teddy pops off heads now. Like grapes. Whole theaters of headless bodies. The police are baffled. He is beyond clothes. Called spouse but could not utter a word. "I know it's you!" she said. And hung up. Things best settled resolutely. Brief stop at flea circus yesterday. Teddy totally tranquilized by the little creatures. Have not watched television at all! I dread the change of life. Sonja Henie was without question a superb ice skater. Teddy...still loves me.

The real hooker is that they are using real combat vets! R.R. has answered Conrad. Puglisi soon out to become Rosenbloom's *aide de camp*.

Teddy is in the latrine. He has been there two hours. He has grown so large he can't get out. He occupies all the space, and the walls are cracking. Soon the street wall will collapse and Teddy will step out. It will be the end for us. I have no hold on him. He is sixteen feet tall and over four thousand pounds.

This movie has everything.

Kong is good. Kong is great.

The Films of R. Nixon

LET ME LIST SOURCES FIRST. THERE ARE TWO THAT MATTER: Abraham Fletner's *Lost Film Empires* (Boise, 1937) and Bukarov's *Minions of the Dream*, translated from the Russian by L. Gaico (Worcester, 1938). Both works appeared in small editions, quickly went out of print, and are now virtually unobtainable. A provocative but much disputed article by Abbie Denton titled "Demonism in Hollywood" appeared in the one-issue-only magazine, *Undergrowth*, published by A. Denton in Cincinnati in 1939. Briefly its thesis was that Hollywood was inhabited by genuine devils, and movies were a conspiracy by the Prince of Darkness to corrupt America. So be it. The *facts* are meager but unassailable. In the years between 1931 and 1938 a young collegian and later law student named R. Nixon, to make ends meet, did bit parts and finally starred in nearly two dozen films by fly-by-night film companies, usually under the name Sirius O'Dell and (at least) twice under the name Camp Mulligan (no doubt some youthful *joi d'esprit*). These companies, run often by madmen, made hundreds of films, most of which have been permanently lost because of poor quality film and poor organization. The films were quickly and cheaply done, made quick profits in third run theaters mostly in the South and Midwest, and disappeared. Fletner, who died mysteriously the same year his book was published, was a fringe critic whose homosexuality, finally, put him beyond the pale. It was his claim that much of America's film heritage was lost with these films, and much credit is due him for preserving so much of what we now have. Bukarov came to America in 1937, after years of study in Germany. He toured the country intensely, seeing (and cataloging) thousands of films, returned to Russia, published, and was thought to be liquidated soon after.

The minor role films are best dealt with first because they

establish a major pattern. There are seven definitely known about: "Trailer Park," "Taxicab Blues," "Ambassador of Love," "Savage Men," "The Goldonki Papers," "Medico on the Move," and "Gnadige Fräulein." There is some speculation about four lost major films (including the fabled "Klondike Ike") and several minor ones, which I shall deal with in a subsequent article to be titled "The Lost Films of R. Nixon."

"Gnadige Fräulein" can be dispensed with most quickly as it was a German propaganda film "destroyed" at the end of World War II by the Russians. Little is know about it. How "Sirius O'Dell" got involved in it is unknown, except that he was on vacation at the time it was filmed (oddly, in California) and played a wounded Jewish war veteran of World War I. He had no lines, but, being grievously wounded, moaned a good deal and appeared unshaven. In "The Goldonki Papers," another excursion into European politics, he appears briefly as a diplomatic courier and is memorable for the line "I shall go to Pinsk!" "Medico on the Move" finds him again injured, this time a high school football player about to have his leg amputated. In a moving scene, thinking he is about to have his leg reset, he asks his doctor, played by the legendary Tyrus Solari, "Can I still play football?" To which Solari, moved by his pluck, answers, "By God, I think you will!" "Trailer Park" gets him on the road, one of a happy band of young vagabonds. Nomadic, much like the gypsies, he and his companions seek fun and adventure throughout the byways of America. Until, stopping one day at dusk by a trailer park, he meets his fate in the shape of sloe-eyed Loretta Banyan, who later, in real life, went on to be the first woman to swim the Gulf of California. As his companions move on to further horizons, he sings his first movie song, "Love Holds Me Down," and ceases his roving. A minor role, but charming.* His next movie, "Ambassador of Love," finds him not as the "ambassador," but as the jilted suitor, and it is much to his credit that most

---

*Some critics feel that "Trailer Park" is really a transition film *between* his minor and major films. However, although Nixon-O'Dell is *visible* throughout much of the movie, his lines are few and his story quite secondary. It is true that he looks *promising*, but that is hardly enough to escape the rubric "minor."

audiences felt that he should have gotten the girl (the fabulous Fay Caroway). "Taxicab Blues" was a musical trifle, but in it he demonstrates that he has nimble feet and again sings, most notably "The Fleet Is In." Far and away the most important of these minor films is "Savage Men." The film is an answer to the question "What happens on a desert isle with twelve men and a girl?" Although he dies early in the film (defending the heroine's honor), it is here, in this brief portrayal, that he manifests the histrionic depth that was to make for a major, however brief and "lost," film career. It can be noted that most of these films have, whether by design or accident, something in common—the young man usually on the losing end of life, love, and fate, but perservering bravely, with dignity, to physical or moral success and capturing the compassion of his audience. Even in "Taxicab Blues," where he appears utterly frivolous, he redeems himself by speeding the pregnant heroine to the hospital despite rush hour traffic, and is rewarded by being first to hold the baby (a girl), to whom he sings Brahms' "Lullabye." It is this theme of rising above life's difficulties that we shall follow in the major films.

Most difficult of the major films to absorb is, of course, "The Gay Blade." Beginning with its title, it is full of peculiar "style" and double entendre which we shall not discuss here. For example, at one point the hero asks himself rhetorically, "Am I my brother's keeper?" and responds, "Maybe. But what of my sister?" What is one to make of that? The hero, a thorough cad, is a swordsman of renown, but equally well known for his boudoir sexploits. He is handsome but fickle. Women love and hate him; men fear him. Under the protection of the infamous Cardinal du Duc he rides roughshod over the women of the empire. His downfall comes when he and the Cardinal clash over the favors of La Belle Roxanne, the empire's first prostitute. The Cardinal, of course, wins out, and our hero barely escapes with his life. But his loss turns out to be his gain. Penniless and hungry, he wanders through the land, meeting the people. He remembers his own poor childhood, his virtuous, hard-working, and widowed mother. He goes to her grave and there weeps. A peasant girl comforts him shyly. He asks her name and takes service with her father, who, as was his own father, is a carpenter. During a brief interlude of peace and harmony he woos and wins the radiant peasant girl, who bears him beautiful and healthy children. But meanwhile the Cardinal has seized power and makes his tyranny felt in every corner of the land. One day, some lecherous soldiers of the Cardinal kill the hero's wife as she resists their advances. Our hero straps sword to his side once more, and with it takes on a new life. He slays the soldiers, becomes a hero of the people, and leads the rebellion, which is successful. Meanwhile, La Belle Roxanne, who has always loved him, is about to take final vows. He bursts in, declares his love, and asks her to rule with him as a virtuous queen. In a final coronation and marriage scene, he speaks to his people. "A thousand years of peace!" he declares, as he winks at La Belle Roxanne. And the people know that the "gay blade" is buried forever and in his place there stands their true monarch.

Another humble-origin-triumphant film is "The Other Side of the Tracks." This film tells it straight. The hero, a Polish boy named Peter Malinski, is the son of a sausage stuffer in Chicago. It is a happy family but money is scarce. Young Peter is frail and frequently the butt of other children's jokes. His father is disappointed in him and buys him a football. But Peter misses the very first throw and gets a bloody nose. Thereafter his father leaves him to his mother and his books. Young Peter does not have the money to buy books and he feels too shabby to go to the public library. So he rummages in garbage cans and trash bins for them. This leads ultimately to his success, for in addition to books young Peter brings home odds and ends which he sells. He soon becomes the first Polish junk dealer in Chicago and buys the sausage factory his father works in, making his father a foreman. He also establishes a free Polish library for neighborhood children, and, disdaining the hand of the sausage factory's former owner's Jewish daughter, he marries the young English librarian he has imported for his Free Polish Library. The movie ends touchingly with Peter and his father tossing a football in front of the sausage factory, which is also their front yard. They are both laughing.

"Burst Bubble" is the last of these direct proletarian films. It is the first business musical in films and R. Nixon's first musical of any kind (if we do not consider his brief role in "Taxicab Blues" and his song in "Trailer Park"). The hero in this film starts at the top. He is a stockbroker, and opens the film tap-dancing down lower Broadway and singing "I Love Wall Street," the refrain of which goes

> I love Wall Street;
> I love the money jingle.
> I love Wall Street;
> It makes my spine tingle.

In swift sequence there follow: 1. a high pressure Wall Street day, with executive lunch ("It's a Deal, It's a Deal"), 2. dinner with a fabulous beauty (Gloria Panaki, who died of blood-poisoning immediately after the film was made*), 3. a Broadway opening ("Give Me the Great White Way"), followed by cocktails with the cast in a club, and 4. a moonlit buggy ride through Central Park. The role is acted with *panache*, and several song and dance numbers, particularly "You Give Me Goose Pimples" and "I Wish This Night Would Never End" (lyrics in both by Bennie "the Turk" Capabella), are memorable. But disaster, of course, strikes. The stock market crashes, and our hero is reduced to pounding the pavement for work. No more song and dance. No more executive lunch. That is, until one day, as he is wiping his sweaty head, a girl (the Irish actress Irena Clay-Fitz) drops a dime in his hat. "Hey," he says, "weren't you my secretary?" In response to which she does a little tap dance. He joins in, their feet doing all the talking. Then they sing "The Good Old Days," joined by a chorus of jobless men and women. Suddenly it is raining dimes from heaven, and the mob scrambles for them. But the hero and his secretary are left with only the dime in his hat. They share the same cup of coffee, a touching and sensuous scene with close focus on lips and tongues

---

*Gloria Panaki may well have been the originator of the bunny tail, for in an earlier film, "Hat Check Girl," she appears briefly—and devastatingly—with cotton candy stuck to her backside.

and eyes, and she declares, pregnantly, a speck of coffee dripping from her mouth, "You know, I'm still your secretary, if you want me." There is a baffled pause. "But I have no money," he says. "Then get it," she answers. And, as if a light has gone on in his head, he leaps off his stool and sings

I'll get it.	The money,
I'll get it.	The money,
I'll get it.	The money,
Wherever it is.	Wherever it is.

And he does. By the pailful. His secretary becomes his wife, and he moves from the East Side to Westchester, takes up golf, and starts a family. Memory of the burst bubble fades, but not the impulse to sing and dance. Together at the movie's close (she slightly round at the belly, surely another movie first), they sing and dance their way through "A House, a Wife, and a Cradle," emphasizing what really counts in life.

With "Tahiti Breeze" we are into a different phase entirely. For one thing, our hero appears throughout the film in only a loin cloth. For another, he is colored a Polynesian amber. He is Papu the pearl diver. This film and "Desert Rider" are often called his "ethnic" films for good reason. They explore, indirectly to be sure, the non-Western ambiance and psyche, what we might today call the third world ethos. In "Tahiti Breeze" Papu is strong and independent. He is friends with all the creatures of the sea, even the giant clam, which he knows how to tickle. He lives simply, lolling on the waves, diving for a pearl when he (rarely) needs cloth or trinkets. One day, into Loakua Lagoon, a ship with evil white men comes. They have been invited by the island's greedy Oriental merchant. They have guns and they seek pearls. They enslave and oppress the island people, all except Papu, who is too wily for them. In particular, a beautiful but bad white woman (played to the hilt by Lola Berkowitz) whips them. Exhausted and frightened, the islanders in desperation kidnap Lola one night and steal away to the demon God Tagaloa, who lives in a volcano. They offer him human sacrifice, the evil white woman, if he will help them. Tagaloa roars and belches fire in pleasure. The island shakes. Suddenly, Papu steps forward. "No," he says in Polynesian. "*Oaku malay toe narooka.*" ("All life is sacred") "*Eeanna no maka rekanga da ook!*" ("I," he says, "shall rid you of the evil ones!") The natives are at first uncertain. Then the girl cries, and they decide to give Papu a chance. He frees her trembling body, which she then heaves into his arms. His eyes light up with new sensation. "*Oaku ba kaga no oopa,*" says one of the tribal elders, and they laugh and move off. The next day, Papu approaches the white men and makes them understand that he can show them where there are giant pearls. Their greed blinds them to his intent and they go with him to his secret lagoon. He insists that they dive down with him, and he shows them that it is harmless to reach into the giant clam. The white men then resurface and dive again, each to a giant clam. And each becomes trapped, for it is only the innocent Papu who can be friend to the clams. The island immediately celebrates, and Papu takes the white woman off to his lagoon, where he discovers that she cannot swim. The film ends with Lola and Papu splashing water on each other and giggling. "*Mee nana gooaka?*" Lola smiles (the island midwives have instructed her; surely one of the great moments in film history). Papu laughs, showing all his teeth, and dives for her. The camera then moves down into the depths and focuses briefly on the half-eaten bodies of the evil white men. Tagaloa has been fed after all.

A much more prophetic and apocalyptic film was "Desert Rider." One of the first on-location films (shot outside Las Vegas), its setting is the desert sheikdoms of the Near East. The film opens on a scene of carnage. Arab is slaughtering Arab. A lone rider comes out of the desert. "Stop!" he shouts. "Desist!" The Arabs do stop fighting, but they seize the lone rider, whose name is Ahmed, and torture him. How, exactly, is unclear, but it is clearly unspeakable. Through it all Ahmed keeps muttering "Let there be peace. Let there be peace." The Arabs finally give up in disgust and leave him to die. But he does not die. He becomes instead a legend. Wherever Arab kills Arab he appears, shouting, "Stop! Desist! Let there be peace!" The Arabs obey him because they do not know whether he is of the living or the dead. He gains power and becomes a great leader, recalling to all Arabs their duties to Allah, cleansing them of their lazy and wicked ways. In one scene (the movie makes no pretense to historical or cultural accuracy) Ahmed whips the semi-naked concubines from a local sheik's harem, urging them to more fruitful ways. Subsequently he unites all Islam to join in battling the "Infidel." "Let there be peace!" he orders, and leads the army eastward. But, while pausing at a small oasis, Ahmed meets a girl who is secretly Christian. A star blazes in the sky, and he is miraculously converted. She proposes marriage, but he says he cannot be her husband for reasons he cannot explain. She says she understands, and leaves him praying for guidance. In the morning he tries to convert a quarter of a million Arabs to Christianity. This time they do not leave him until he is dead. They ride on, soon to squabble again among themselves. The secret Christian comes, washes his face, kisses him, and weeps. As Bach's *Actus Tragicus* thunders from the screen, the camera focuses on pipe lines laid across the desert sands, silent but eloquent testimony that Christianity cannot long be held back.

"Passionella" is a total aberration. Directed by the mad "monk," Izzie Goldfarb, who disappeared in Mexico in 1940, it is unlike any other of R. Nixon's films. It is as if an insanity seized all connected with the venture. Goldfarb's earlier films, especially "The Bird in the Nest" and the insidious "Wanton Finger" with Thrush Soong and "Killer" Jake Begner, give some indication. Leading lady in "Passionella" was Margaret Fahrlarter, notorious six time suicide of the Thirties. Three-fourths of the cast and crew never made another film. The hero, a callow hedonist who might have rowed through life well enough married to the right woman, plunges from depth to depth of sensual excess, always in search of the mysterious Passionella who plagues his dreams. The dream sequences are truly Byzantine. Fahrlarter, a giant of a woman, appears in a variety of orgasmic *couture*—leather, gauze, wax paper, sea weed, soap suds, grease (probably the most exciting), and, once, only in her own ankle length hair. She is the Devil's chief succubus, and in each dream excites O'Dell-Nixon to greater sexual height.

He is drained of his energies and comes, during, before, and after sleep, to dread sleep itself. But there is no escaping it. Finally, in despair he proposes to the plain Priscilla next door. To his horror, she metamorphoses before his eyes into Passionella, her teeth now longer, her hair a raven's black, her body undulating, swollen, and swallowing with Gargantuan desires. She opens her arms to him, and the dream, now life, goes on and on to sensual oblivion. It is a mad film, a lunatic vision, and one can only speculate what effect it had on its leading man. Surely there is some connection between it and Goldfarb's plunge below the border, and with the variety of disasters that befell those connected with it in any way. Fahrlarter, oddly, after her sixth suicide attempt, gave up on it and became a grandmother. One wonders whether, toothless and rocking, she ever remembered that once, long before, she was—Passionella, whose tresses so long drove men mad. Or the haunting and lyrical lines of O'Dell when she first approaches his bed, her robes trailing: "Whence comes this gorgeous pot of flesh? Methinks disaster sweet is soon upon me." Probably not.

Shocking, but never to the extent of "Passionella," and mitigated by being more rooted in literature and myth, was "Till Death Do Us Part," a retelling of the Bluebeard legend. Set in Victorian Boston (though filmed in San Francisco), O'Dell works his way through seven women, each one of a different ethnic background. He disposes of them by knife, axe, pitchfork, rope, snake, horse, and (unbelievably) sausage. He is suave and demented, a perfect gentleman and lover until that certain point. And then—they go, some quietly, some shrieking and kicking (one, the Abyssinian, actually laughing hysterically). The film lacks the sociological inference of earlier films, and its psychological substratum is spurious. One cannot help imagining that it was something of a lark to do, for one can detect a certain humorous glint in the hero's eyes at the film's most (truly) awful moments. For example, when wife number five, a Spanish dancer, announces on what is to be *the* night that she is tired, he responds, quite drolly, "Oh, what a pity, my dear." The pitchfork is waiting upstairs. It is interesting here to wonder whether among the lost films there might not be a comedy.

Finally, "Wings of the Monarch" (which some prefer to consider a "lost" film) and "Man in Space." "Wings of the Monarch" was released only in the northeast corner of Wisconsin and there are, *as of this date*, no known copies. Relatively few people saw it, and knowledge of its content depends mainly on the memories of a few old women. A Mrs. Clara Crump of Bartonville says that it was the most moral, most impressive film she had ever seen. However, she must be confused because she remembers it as a cowboy film whereas it was clearly an historical film about a Cromwell-like figure in the Middle Ages. Harriet Bently, also of Bartonville, says only that he (O'Dell) was "gorgeous" and "divine." The consensus seems to be that it was a magnificent acting job, that the film was studded with overtones of relevance, that it was inspirational, and that it ended tragically. Nothing beyond that can be said with certainty. A few years ago it was asserted that the film was a version of *Piers Plowman*, but that notion was thoroughly discredited recently by a graduate student in Omaha. In a way, it is unfortunate that "Man in Space" was not lost instead of "Wings of the Monarch," for it is very much a disaster. An obvious and trivial attempt to keep pace with the modern world, the film creaks in all its parts. The hero at the controls of his spaceship looks very much like Papu in his outrigger canoe. The film is full of gimmicks, the outer space scenes comparing unfavorably with Oz. Very briefly there is romantic interest when the hero encounters a long-haired space creature called Kroxin ("*Na ook kana goo oolu*," the hero says at their first encounter), but it is a hermaphrodite, and attention quickly dwindles. The hero's name is Kro-Narch,* and he is forever checking his situation with "base," which flashes pictures of his smiling wife and family to him regularly from their bubble house. Kro-Narch succeeds finally in negotiating an arms treaty which limits each global sphere to six trillion mega-tons of "fusion" bombs. He returns to earth a hero and has breakfast at the White House (in his space suit).

---

*For several years this was the name of a popular cereal among blacks in the rural South. It was the cereal of "go-getters" and "comers."

Such, then, are the currently known films of R. Nixon. It is to be regretted that no "western" film yet exists, nor any comedy. Undoubtedly, his career in film could have continued had he wished it. (A clique of professors in New England believes that it did continue.) As it is, there is a sufficient body of work upon which to build considerable analysis and speculation, which will be the subject of a third essay, tentatively entitled "The Deep Image in The Films of R. Nixon." Suffice it to say at the present time that in any study of his work, the starting point must be, as indicated in this brief survey, the continuing metaphor of the poor boy (peon, peasant, slave, the disinherited, modern man) rising above the difficulties of environment (class, evil, society, heredity, life itself, God) to power and success. A study of the directors of these films, particularly Goldfarb and Neidermander (Can anyone ever forget his "Fly in the Ointment"?), serves to confirm this insight. R. Nixon-O'Dell-Mulligan by any consideration must be considered one of the significant actors of his time and his films an archive of cultural insight.

The Whitman Lesson

THE FOLLOWING IS SPOKEN IN A GERMAN ACCENT WITH A certain heavy-handed melodrama: "I schmear you with *may*onaisse. I put you in *roll*. I exhibit you in museum with title *Good Looking Hot Dog!*" You say "Hah! Hah! I am pretzel in disguise! You are loving me not so easy!" All this during a class I am teaching with you. You have been putting on airs, condescending, and I say what I say to put you in your place. You are startled. You don't know what to say. (?) You are tempted to laugh but do not because you are afraid the laugh might be on you. The other students laugh at first, then are silent. They think I might be crazy. I wear a suit and tie and have never spoken like this before. I am pleased.

The next day everyone is waiting. The totally unexpected is in the air. I sense you are apprehensive, a bit fearful. If I could say what I said, I could do anything, I am *unpredictable*. I let the quiet grow. I am aware of the curve of your legs, your hidden breasts (more hidden today, I think). "Walter Whitman," I begin, "is not what you think he is. And by the way—" suddenly Hitlerian, staring straight at her—"In your *armpits* I am pouring *ketchup, piccalilly, horse radish!* and then schmearing all over with *salt, pepper, French dressing, French fries, MUSTARD*. Where not am I schmearing, *hah? hah?*" She does not appear to answer today. She looks, in fact, terrified, Rhine blond though she is. "There will not be any discussion," I continue, "of whether or not Walt was a fag. It is immaterial." And then, in a strained falsetto, "In my nookie you are not schmearing because there is a trap! He, he, he. A trap which is catching you in Strauss waltz. He, he, he." I sigh quietly. Engagement at last. The battle joined. The flames lick at me. We spend the rest of the period discussing "The Children of Adam" in strange and somber silence.

The next morning we are up to "Calamus," root poems, stalks, tendrils, all manner of bullshit. She has dealt with her fear, swallowed it, sits now with a sassy slack look, her legs, sheathed in tight denim, spread—interestingly. "In your mouth," she purrs, "I am putting chopped grasshoppers with molasses. In your *nose*, scraping from the tongue of pig, mixed with crushed pregnant fly, and *garlic salt!*" "Ahh, ahh," I say, "you are hot tomato Bavarian baby." "*Nein! Nein!*" she shrieks. "I am pig schnott in your ear! I am putting *gas* in your *grosse behindt. Schnell! Schnell!*" And with that I make my concluding remarks on "Song of Myself," Levine himself it is, going down.

The class has become quite excited about Whitman. They have taken my advice and begun reading him aloud in private, letting out all the rant. (It is my recommendation for Milton also.) *I* have taken to sitting on my desk, which is really a four by six table, and very sturdy. *She* now sits on the edge of her chair, her dresses skirting up. A good many in the class look at her legs, and she is getting crowded. I am one hundred percent zippered, but have thought about it (?) a good deal. Today is "When Lilacs Last in the Dooryard Bloomed" and "Passage to India." "*Sauerkraut!*" I leer at her. "*Wurst! Wurst!*" her lips pout back. "*Sauerbrauten!*" I moan, "hot *schpice*, flowers *schtuffed* in you." "Mine nookie," she coos, "is not talkink today. He, he, he." We all know she doesn't mean it. Her hand, for example, is between her legs, and she is smiling her lewd Bavarian smile. "*Nookie iss kraut in der ungerschpassen gedankt,*" I say. I don't know a word of German. "*Yah. Yah,*" she drawls, "*in springt der clippenbord, das gewassen zunkt.*" I leap off the table, and that is that. *Enden. Fire.* Next class is Hawthorne, and that, *grâce à dieu!* is another matter entirely.

Dirty Old Man

LET ME TELL YOU ABOUT A STRANGE THING I SAW ON THE
subway last week. I am a very regular rider of the subway. I find
that it fits reasonably well into the routine of my life, and I take its
difficulties in my stride. Sometimes I get a seat, sometimes I do not;
sometimes its air blowers work, sometimes they do not; and
usually I get where I want when I want. There is also reasonable
diversion for an alert mind. The advertisements, for example,
which are a fascinating study of our society. One can even perform
certain inconspicuous exercises to keep trim, such as tightening and
loosening one's buttocks. Most of all there are the people. I am an
inveterate observer of people, a Peeping Tom on humanity, if you
like. Sometimes I think I must be a little excessive because I do not
merely look, I *feast* myself on people. Other riders read their
newspapers passionately or retreat nimbly inside themselves or
sleep. Very few look. And no one looks as greedily as I do. It is as if
there were a great secret I must uncover. My looking is usually
connected with fantasy. With women, I strip them naked and dwell
on their possibilities of pleasure. How large their nipples, for
example, or the thickness of their pubic hair. I look right through
the clothing and come to my conclusions. With men, I mostly
compare. Are they more self-assured than I, more successful in
love, more impressive? Are they men of power and brilliance?
Would they be hostile to me? Or are they obviously lesser creatures
than I? Can I safely pity them for their shabby lives and shabby
souls? Sometimes I go over the edge into violence and mutilate men
for their arrogance, their total lack of humility. It is insufferable
that any man would dare to belittle me, or laugh at me, or fail to
take note of me. It is not even beyond me to kill with the proper
provocation. I have wondered whether any of this ever showed on
my face, whether my sighs or grunts were more than vividly

imagined. It is difficult to say, for although I have great control over my facial expression, finding a bland look the least troublesome in most situations, were my fantasies to break through, no one would tell me. I once saw a teenage boy suddenly begin barking and snapping at people like a wolf. He was very serious about it. But he was totally ignored. A few people found a way to change their position very inconspicuously. But no one challenged him directly with his state. Had he urinated or defecated on them it would have been the same. Anyway, as I said, I feast on humanity; I gorge myself. And one day last week I was staring at an attractive girl in her early twenties. She was not ravishingly beautiful in her face, though its serenity and classic features made it most acceptable. But her body was irresistible. All the more so because she seemed so unaware of its irresistibility. It was, so to speak, waiting (quite selflessly) for sensual recognition; and I was ravaging it. Her face had the same quality. It was quiet, quiescent, but with full soft lips waiting to be touched, pressed, tasted, sucked, bitten. And one knew they would come alive, for their tranquility was not the result of stupidity, nor neurosis. They were simply something that had somehow ripened, like the rest of her, far too much without anyone seeing. And now all of her hung there, lusciously, maddeningly, for me. Yes, for me. In all truth, it should have been unsafe for her to appear in public in that condition. My absorption was total. But it was not, I soon discovered, uncontaminated. Sitting next to the girl was an old man. His mouth was freshly stained; from tobacco, possibly wine, I suppose. His head was sweaty, he needed a shave, he was unclean. On his face was the fat, silly grin of a senile man, and in his lap his left hand quivered from some disease. It was the hand that interfered with my concentration and pleasure. It seemed to have a life of its own. I could not ignore its insistent quivering. In fact, I saw the hand before I saw that its owner was staring at the girl with gross lust. And his eyes were not silly at all. They were hard, direct, and cold. I could see him inhaling all her smells, from the slightly stale perfume to the sweet sweaty flesh of her clinging thighs. He was obviously a connoisseur (still), despite the jelly brains in his head. Once or twice he looked at me; in derision, I thought. But I looked away. I hated him immediately, both because of what he was doing and because of his image, which to me was that of an end product to a lifetime of self-indulgence and debauchery. That he should be violating her was so ugly, so unsuitable, so grotesque. All I can say in mitigation was that she was oblivious of him and his stench also. We rode like that for several stations, people coming and going, the steady rumble of the train beneath me. I still sucked her in, but now self-consciously, with an eye also for the old man lest he catch me at my pleasure. I was aware somehow that it was a strangely unresolved situation. Several things bothered me. For example, if I got off before either of them, I would never know what happened. Of course, *nothing*, but the point was I would never know. If either he or the girl got off first, things would not be so bad. And if they both got off together before I did, well. . . . But no one got off at all, and I confess I became anxious, for my station was coming up soon. The old man himself gave our situation a definite configuration, the very thing that has been troubling me since. Just as the train was leaving one station, he lifted his trembling hand from his lap and put in on her thigh. I hate clichés, but quite literally I could not believe my eyes. My heart pounded and I held my breath. Never in all my experience had such a thing happened. The girl at first seemed not to notice, and I thought that, typically, she was going to avoid this unpleasantness by refusing to recognize it. But then, as he slowly moved his hand up under her dress, she turned to him with something like shock and disbelief in her face. It was rather like a rude and unexpected awakening. I have to give him credit for courage. He was looking straight at her with his hard eyes. And though his face had dissolved into a face of youthful idiocy, his eyes had a bizarre power in them. I could tell she was affected. I was not sure whether she did not do anything immediately because she was afraid, confused, or whatever. It is even possible that in some remote way she recognized him. I thought, very briefly, perhaps he is a crazy relative from the old country, and then realized how ridiculous the idea was. All I can say definitely is that she met his gaze, recognized the power there, and was silent. And during all these *seconds* he continued to move his hand upward. I became quite excited. I could see her undergarment (pale blue), see his fingers slide under and reach in. And at the same time, her legs going perceptibly slack, the look of shock was blended into a look of awkward but not unwelcome pleasure. She had gorgeous legs. Slim as they had seemed below (and shapely), up near her undergarment they were incredibly full and fleshy and white. And there where his hand, now no longer trembling, was clutching and opening rhythmically, there it seemed an unbelievable nest of sweetness and joy. At some point (unperceived by me) I had ceased to hate the old man and had begun to share with him a pleasure I could never have instigated myself. For even though I was a poor second, still I was getting so much more than I had ever imagined. I was supremely thrilled. If only, I thought, he would *rip off her pants*. I realized that at any moment I would have to leave because the next stop was mine. What could possibly justify my remaining? Surely it would be apparent to everyone why I was lingering. The girl's legs were now quite obviously spread. She had slid down in her seat and leaned to one side as the old man worked away with ferocious concentration. She was drooling, and with a lazy smile she muttered, "Dirty old man, *kiss me!*" Words that have been burned into me and shock me unbearably. She began to squeeze her breast, and I saw a hard nipple pressing against her garment. As the train pulled into the station the old man reached over with his other hand and began pulling down her pants. I was furious that it was my stop, and just as I exited I saw a breathtaking expanse of soft white belly with a dark fringe on the bottom. It was sheer madness, and I clutched myself painfully in the groin as I shouldered my way onto the platform. I walked slowly so as to peek in when the train left. But I saw little. It was already going too fast, and he was far too hunched over her. And he laughed, a weird, piercing goatlike laugh, almost of triumph, as he passed me. I was certain he was laughing at me. I thought of various expedients, such as getting a cab and racing two or three stops ahead and getting back on the train. But it was all very problematical. I didn't know how much money I had. There would be no cab handy, or there would be too many red

lights, or there would be a line at the token booth and I would miss
the train, or they would already have gotten off. I can safely say
that I was quite confused as I walked up into the street. The
memory of that ride has caused me great discomfort. I find I am
regularly getting on the same train at the same time, hoping to see
her again. But what good would it do? Would I even recognize her?
And if I did and sat next to her and put my hand on her thigh she
would scream or slap me. I should be arrested and exposed in the
newspapers. I therefore keep returning to the specific occasion
itself. What if *that* day I had not gotten off at my stop? What if I had
taken advantage of her *with* the old man?...What *did* happen? *What
did happen?* I cannot escape that question. Who was that old man and
what was his disease that made his hand tremble so? I feel
profoundly cheated and profoundly mutilated in my soul. I have
been robbed of the sweetest of mysteries. *She should have let me know I
could touch her!* She didn't have to put up with a senile dirty old man.
God damn him to hell!

George Washington's Birthday

YESTERDAY WAS GEORGE WASHINGTON'S BIRTHDAY. I MADE a silly mistake and noted somewhere that today was his birthday. You see, yesterday was a Sunday, so his birthday is celebrated today. I have no interest in George Washington's birthday. We have too many holidays. I do not even celebrate my own birthday. Why should I? Soon enough I shall be dead. I do not like to be reminded. When I was a child, my mother celebrated my birthdays religiously. The early ones were parties, with a few friends and presents. As I got older, we went out together to a restaurant, and then to some entertainment. When I was twelve she died, and then nobody celebrated my birthday. A few aunts sent cards with thin one dollar bills in them, always signing them "With love, Aunt_____." When I was eighteen I made an attempt at a celebration. I invited a few friends, but I did not tell them what it was for. I had a cake, and I laughed a lot. They were confused. It was not a success. After that I pretty much ignored it. However, what I did do for several years was to celebrate my mother's birthday. Of course I had to do it alone. I made a point of rising late and taking a leisurely bath. I then dressed, ate a very light breakfast, and strolled several hours in some lovely place, like a botanic garden, after which I went to a superior restaurant and dined. The afternoon was spent in some activity of an edifying nature. Then home to a brief supper by candlelight, a book, and bed. For a while it was my most perfect day of the year. The only person who ever knew about this celebration was a stranger, an older man. He was sitting at a table next to me one year and wished me a good appetite. I replied that I expected to eat heartily as it was my mother's birthday. "Oh?" he asked. "And where is the good lady?" "She's dead," I replied. "She's been dead over fifteen years." We had no more to say to each other. I can't say that I liked the man. Shortly after, I ceased celebrating even my mother's birthday. I could not remember her very well. There did not seem much point in it. I took no notice of special occasions. Just once, some time later, I was invited to my father's funeral. It was a formality. He had divorced my mother many years ago. I felt like an uncle to his new children. His wife seemed much too young, even with her grief. They cried a good deal, shook my hand, and introduced me to their relatives. My father was quite emaciated. It was a well organized and tasteful funeral. I never saw them again.

Preparations

I TEND TO BECOME ABSORBED WITH POSSIBILITIES OTHER people find absurd. For example, what if the telephone rings while you are standing naked after a shower? Come quick, your child is unconscious. She is a block away. She has a chronic illness. You know what she needs. What do you do? Take the medication you need and rush over naked? Or take the extra minute to put on clothes? Which might be a fateful minute: you arrive dressed but too late. Put it in all its variations—you are making love, in conference, on the toilet, late for an appointment, about to eat: *somebody needs you at once*—the vast majority of mankind would arrive too late. Yet what good citizen, yourself included, would hesitate to smile at the man or woman who ran naked through the street? It simply is not done.

Obviously I am not talking nonsense. But thinking this way does make nonsense of my life. Looking at friends, I wonder, "Would you rush naked to my dying side?" It is, of course, like much else, a metaphor. There are many ways to be naked. How many, and which, trivial things come between you and life? Are they really trivial? Are they perhaps life itself (which would require some serious rethinking)? But people do die. Terrible things do happen. Thus much of my internal life is spent *rehearsing* what I would do in certain circumstances. And I confess that I find myself wanting. I am forced to pay more attention to certain *small* things about myself (You can well imagine what) and take my measure anew. And, in a philosophical way, I am aghast, I mutter, I smile even—how odd life is, what a coward I am, what a solid member of society.

I came to these reflections upon hearing of a certain Ukrainian woman I had seen around, a wife, illiterate. Her husband had heart trouble but was getting along. Friends were visiting, former students, a colleague. She was in the bedroom, changing. There was a loud knock: "Anya! Come quick! It's Fred!" (He was not Russian.) She came out instantly and rushed to the parlor. She was wearing only her underpants. She was fifty-five, much over-weight, not pretty. Her breasts hung. Her stomach revealed its folds. Under her arms, at her back, was fat. She went to her husband, knelt, spoke maybe ten words which no one heard, and he died. Of course, I thought, a peasant. She could do that. It didn't matter. But that was not so. She was, I found out, illiterate only in English, was, in fact, quite educated, had even, in her youth, published a book of poems. And that bothered me, as well as a number of other things. I might as well list them. They have no order.

1. What language did she speak to him in, and did it matter? Did Fred understand Russian? Is it possible that he did not understand Russian, that she nevertheless spoke in Russian, and that it was right that she did so, that is, that Fred heard more and better because he did not understand and died with as much grace as possible? (What language did she use when they made love— There is a question here, but irrelevant.)

2. Obviously, had she put on a bathrobe, her husband would have been dead when she got to him. Would it have mattered, and if so, how much, and to whom? Not to Fred, certainly. The great evaders of life would no doubt quibble in this matter, missing the point entirely, e.g., she could have put on her bathrobe in transit, so to speak.

3. The people there (some were female)—they must have been shocked, perhaps more so at her nakedness than Fred's death. Did they find her gross? Ludicrous? Obscene? Would it have been easier for them had she been younger, slimmer, firmer, prettier?

4. Did Fred see their disgust at her nakedness? Was he, also, perhaps shocked? Did he appreciate the extraordinary swiftness, I might even say nakedness, of her response? Or would he have preferred to die more decorously, unspoken to by a fat and naked wife in full view of students, colleagues, friends?

5. When Anya finally got up, did she look at any of them? Did *she*

77

suddenly feel naked? How did she walk out, as she must have, to get dressed (some things we always finish, if we live)? Did any one of them touch her, put an arm over her, perhaps hold her? Did anyone think to cover her, and if so, did she think, how *ridiculous*, he is *dying*! May you choke on my flesh!

6. Was she sweating? Or was she cold as ice? Did she smell?

7. What had she looked like when young? Were there children? Why had I, before this incident, thought her a peasant? Why wasn't her English better? What were her poems about? Had they been translated?

8. The incident, I am sure, is etched inside the skulls of those who were privileged to bear witness. Does it remain sharp-edged, uncomfortable, troubling? Do they keep up the relationship? Do they avoid her, drop her? Does she retreat to her *Russians*, her language family? If she had been *completely* naked, could they have lived, on any terms, with the memory? (What is the memory of those who hear the sounds and see the bodies of the mutilated of the world?)

9. How do they retell the story? What recedes, what becomes highlighted? Do they laugh more with each retelling? Or does the sour taste remain? Do they wonder about their own deaths, who will or will not be present, and why? Will they, the next time, be amongst the dying, the present, or the absent?

This woman is a mystery to me. She has something I do not have, and I do not know why. She had come to her dying husband and grasped his heart in her raw hand. It is the nature of civilization, of any culture, in fact, to interpose *things* (clothing, manners, systems of thought) between people and *life*, by which I mean the hidden life that simmers or bubbles beneath the surface like some molten pool out of dim time. The savage, I realize, is no different from me. Reduction is everywhere the law, perhaps the necessary law: there is no game without it. I wear my clothes; the savage carries his feather or magic pebble. We both suffer grievous loss for it; sometimes we even die for it. Only individuals escape, but who they are, how and why, I do not know. But I recognize their superiority, as I recognize the tragic limits and realness of my own *hesitations*: the measure of any civilization is in its hesitations, its pauses, its reservations. Outside of them is wildness, lawlessness, that is as frightening and lonely as it is free. And it is there that Anya is situated.

I have come to bear her a kind of cosmic love. I do not speak to her, but I have made certain modifications in my life to accommodate her existence. They are modest, to be sure, but I think they move in the right direction. For example, I don't sleep as well. It is conscious, on my part. I am deliberately more likely to awaken at a moment's notice. I am not about to go running anywhere *naked*, with my backside, so to speak, unwiped, but I definitely sleep less well. And, oddly, I *dream* much more. Also, I eat differently. For years, it was my custom, when the telephone rang at dinner, to have my wife answer and say we were eating, could they call back. For a while I considered leaving it off the hook at dinner but thought my regular callers might eventually feel rebuffed. But now, when it rings, my wife (who is watching me carefully) says, "Just a moment," and there I am, quickly swallowing my microcosm of food, ready for whatever it is. It is trivial, perhaps even silly, yet I feel *proud*, a little more than proud, possibly a bit mad. If ever I were to die, it would be so comforting to me to have fat Anya, naked, kneeling, hovering over me, sweating like a pig, muttering incomprehensible guttural sweet Russian to me. If I could speak, I would answer, oh, so happily, "*Yes. Yes. I know. You are right. Hold me, Anya.*" And it would be all right.

Sister Francetta and the Pig Baby

LET ME GET RIGHT INTO IT. WHEN SISTER FRANCETTA WAS A little girl she looked into a baby carriage one day and saw a baby with a pig head. It wore dainty white clothes, had little baby hands and feet, a baby's body. Of course the sounds it made were strange, but the main thing was the pig head. It lay there on its back, kicking its feet, waving its arms, and staring at the world through a pig head. Now Sister Francetta taught us her morality through stories. For example, little boys and girls who put their fingers in forbidden places sometimes found that their fingers rotted away. That was the moral of a story about a boy who picked his nose. However, rotting fingers were a comparatively mild consequence. Sister Francetta's childhood world was filled with sudden and horrible attacks of blindness, deafness, and dumbness. Ugly purple growths developed overnight anywhere inside or outside of people's bodies. Strange mutilations from strange accidents were common. It absolutely did not pay to be bad. Sinful thoughts were the hardest to protect against. Prayer and confession were the surest remedies. As I grew older, Sister Francetta's tales gradually subsided into remote pockets of my mind, occasionally to crop up in dream or quaint reminiscence. Except for the pig baby. The pig baby is still with me. It was different from her other stories. For example, it had no moral, it was just there: there had once been a baby with a pig head. Also, whereas Sister Francetta told her other stories often, and with variations, she told the story of the pig baby only once. And she told it differently, as if she herself did not understand it but nevertheless felt a tremendous urgency to reveal it. The other stories she told because they were *useful*. The story of the pig baby she told because she had *faith* in it. It captured my imagination totally. I tried to find out more, but she usually put me off. And I thought a great deal about it. Since Sister Francetta is dead now, I suppose I am the only expert in the world on the pig baby, and what I know can be listed very quickly:

1. The pig baby was apparently Caucasian.

2. Its parents were proud of it and in public seemed totally unaware of its pig head.

3. I do not know how long it lived. It apparently never went to school.

4. It always snorted noticeably but never let out any really piglike sounds like *oink*.

5. It ate and drank everything a regular baby ate and drank.

6. Its parents were not Catholic.

7. Everyone pretended not to notice that the baby had a pig head. For some reason it was not talked about either.

8. At some early point the family either moved away or disappeared.

9. No one said anything about that either.

Sister Francetta died a few years after I had her as a teacher. She was still young. It was whispered among us that she had horrible sores all over her body. I became an excellent student and went on to college. There I developed more sophisticated ideas about the pig baby, the two most prominent of which were 1. that Sister Francetta herself was the pig baby, and 2. that the pig baby was Jesus Christ. There is no logic to either conclusion. Since college I have more or less given up the pig baby. Nevertheless it is a fact that I never look into a carriage without a flush of anxiety. And I cannot get rid of the feeling that Sister Francetta is angry with me.

Rescheduling

I HAVE A PROBLEM. IT IS ESTIMATED THAT I HAVE A GOOD twenty years to live (and an undisclosed number of bad ones). And there are certain things I would like to accomplish. However, I have made mistakes in my past, wasted time, failed to lay foundations and so on. For example, I would like to read reasonably well in Latin, French, German and Italian, and ploddingly in Greek and Russian. But I studied only a little Spanish in my youth and have forgotten even that. To follow the necessary discipline to learn even two of those languages would take at least five years of my spare time. Yes, spare time. For I work, I have family responsibilities. I am no longer a carefree student. And in addition to languages I have ambitions in philosophy, history, art and literature. I am content to let subjects like psychology, music and anthropology slide. Even so, to read history well, one needs a mass of data at one's fingertips— the succession of kings and queens, major battles, treaties, the deeds of great movers and shakers. With such a base, the seeds of historical scholarship fall on fertile ground. But my historical knowledge is helter-skelter, with appalling gaps. Masses of infor- mation drop into deep holes, never to be seen again. You will notice I've not mentioned mathematics or science, not because I don't have a burning desire to follow the latest physics into the macro- and microsphere or penetrate the hieroglyphics of formulae, but because they are simply out of the question. Twenty years full time would barely make me literate there. And even should I do it, I should still be a primitive, for new modes fall like rain everywhere. Some little man would wake up one morning and undo all my work with a simple statement like "One thing is not another." Let us say I could manage a book a week, with two weeks off for holidays, illness, etc. That would be fifty a year or a thousand in twenty years. It seems hardly enough, perhaps not worth the effort. Even with forty good years, I have only two thousand books. And which books? How should they be divided? Were I to read, say, all the major epics of the world or all the novels of Sir Walter Scott, Charles Dickens, Balzac and Henry James, there would be a hundred or so right off the bat, so to speak. This is not to say they are all necessary. Obviously not. But it illustrates the problem. And they are only literature. One could spend five years, maybe more, reading nothing but the collected letters of the major romantic poets in English. My mind collapses at the thought of this. Then there is the large problem of whether one should progress magisterially on all fronts at once, like an armada against the wind, or shoot back and forth from writer to writer, period to period, discipline to discipline. The one is formidable and discouraging in its Pleistocene slowness, the other perhaps maddening in its grass-hoppery skittering. Obviously with the right parents and tradition, with wealth, health, disposition, maturity and luck I would have had all these books resting upon a continent of easy knowledge, the increments piling up smoothly instead of like squalls and flash floods. At times it seems to me that any such plan, given the debacle of my past and the stalemate of my present, is idiocy—something like closing the barn door after the griffins and basilisks have escaped. A far better plan would be to accept my condition with late Melvillian stolidity, make no far-flung plans except, perhaps, to buy a burial plot, concentrating not on goals so much as process. If we may say that death focuses the mind wonderfully, I think we may say also that process is a great comfort. For example, I know people who are very happy because they have managed to merge with the flow of things. My problem here is that I get bogged down in it too much. I read a book twice, three times, because I do not understand it. I say, what is the difference, it is all time well spent, depth is all. But is it? Do I indulge, even delude myself? Several months ago I decided that any educated person should have read Dante, even though I am aware that it is quite possible that Dante could be irrelevant next year, for various reasons. Of course the Italian was out, but I mouthed it anyway, and felt a few aesthetic twitches. The English, unfortunately, seemed banal. And I got botched in the commentaries. I never finished. My only point is, should one spend a year or two or six of one's remaining twenty in reading Dante? Is Dante only for one's remaining forty? And what about Karl Marx? Or Sigmund Freud (not a psychologist, in my opinion)? Or all of Asia and the Third World? What about Kierkegaard or the pre-Socratics? I don't know. Maybe some writers are only for the bad years after the good ones. I suppose one could protect oneself by becoming, exclusively, the world's expert on Camus's North African years, or Phrygian inscriptions, and put everything in suitable perspective. "Your son is dead? A suicide? Interesting. Did you know that in 1938, in Oran, Camus..." That doesn't appeal to me. Last week I read no book at all. That is not quite true. I read several bad ones, because I was sick. I thought I was developing a cancer somewhere in my intestinal tract. It turned out to be something much less serious. That is, whatever it was, it went away. No matter. When I am sick I cannot read serious books, only books that soothe, divert or put me to sleep. But illness is only part of it. I have family crises, holidays during which I must buy gifts, I socialize to a small degree (still a waste), I talk to my wife. I spend too much time reading the newspapers. As if it mattered. And I eat and sleep, of course, and a dozen other daily things. Just going to the bank is a slice in my flesh. Ask me a month later about a particular book and my mind could be a blank. That is because it has no suitable place to rest in my head, no long-time neighbors or established community. My efforts in that area seem far less potent than when I was a youth. Then, things seemed to stick to me as if I were covered with honey. Now my efforts seem more like tubercular rhonchi on a cold night. There is no clearing in my chest. I have books lying all over my home. I am gaining a little weight. I snap at my children, particularly because they don't listen to me. My God, how they waste their time, eating, talking about nothing, listening to sentimental music about lazy dull people. What I need is a fountain of youth. My friends joke and say that I need a second honeymoon. They must be mad. They talk of honeymoons, and I think of hospitals and coffins. For a while, secretly, I thought I would get into superb physical shape, and then I recalled the prisoner in a Russian story who did so before he was hanged. Did he swing the better for it? It really all boils down to the fact that I am stuck, stuck in this life of mine, and there is no getting out of it. I don't even consider that I have probably been a fool most of my life, that I could have made better choices in love, in friends, in my degree of daring. The times I have cowered before trivia! Forget all that. I am content to say I have been in many ways a jack-ass. But I do deplore my *ignorance*, the sad state of my rudderless mind. No doubt others more favored than I similarly deplore on a higher level. That doesn't help me with my problem, namely what to do with my twenty years, how to organize myself for—*what*? My wife still interests me because she is my friend. She has been through it with me. My children are strangers. To them I am a raving aborigine. I don't know one pleasure machine from another. Indeed, I am profoundly unsmiling. No doubt if I am granted a deathbed scene they will shake hands and have a brief shudder of insight. If I can manage it, I would like to laugh, and then go out like a light. ·

The Maldive Chronicles

An Introduction

IT IS PRESUMPTUOUS OF ME TO WRITE AN INTRODUCTION. The very word implies logic, coherence, balance. I claim none of them. Not that I do not admire them. I do. I have always tried to reduce the chaos of existence to order, to plumb the murky pits of life with method. Yes, that is the key to my character: method. But I am too unsettled, too feverish. The readings have all been bad for days. I am in great despair. And great happiness, too. What I mean is that I have been flushed out of myself with truth. But that truth is horrifying. Tomorrow I may be dead. I shall answer the knock, speak my few words, and then offer myself to the mercy of God. Yes, God. Perhaps it is not mercy, but I am certain, now at this moment, that it is God. In finding myself I have found Him. What does it matter if He is a shark, a tiger, a hawk? There is glory to the victim, too. Perhaps Priam knew this when he saw the blood all around him. Oh, Gods! I can hear him shriek. Yes. Well, what about it? What about God? I don't really know. Contradictory? Perhaps. The worst thing about my method is that it yields confusion instead of light. My dissection leads to obfuscation, and my obfuscation to fear. My fear leads to...That is the question. Madness? I have not overlooked that possibility. Perhaps my method is wrong. Perhaps all method is wrong. But I am no philosopher. More precisely, I distrust philosophy. It seems ultimately so refined and hopeless. Do I know? Do I see? Am I here? Am I? Prove it. Yes, well...Prove what? Spell it first, please. Give me the root. How is your Latin and Greek? Do you see my problem? I am almost afraid to breathe. If I exist at all, it is more likely as a voice. Yes, think of me as a voice, a disembodied voice, a rhythmic pattern of sound conveying a mood, a meaning, an essence. I don't think I worry so much about whether God is, but rather, if He is, *does He love me?* Yes, I admit it. I need love. I love love. I bloom, I blossom under love. Melinda—Well, I shall come to her later. She was beautiful. I have gathered together all my notes. They do not make sense. I don't see how I could have said some of the things I did. Perhaps I have died and been reborn. I don't know that other person. Clever. You see, I'm a liar. I am also a thief, a cheat, a boaster, a coward, a lover, and a philanthropist. I do know him. I am a million shells, one within another, enclosing a brilliant jewel (or is it just a brown stone?). Am I the shells or the jewel? I am convinced that if I shattered myself into infinite pieces, someone would at the last moment steal my precious core. But this is all a conceit. It means nothing. I am a consummate sentimentalist. Tomorrow Mrs. Maldive will come. I am sure. That is my fact. And I want to explain. I want someone to know. It is all thrown together, but somewhere in my scraps there is the truth. It is shining. Perhaps only like a light under a door—but shining. Look for it. Study it. I may be dead.

Where I Lived and What For

THE STREET IS McCOOMB STREET. DUTCH, I THINK, BUT NO Dutch live here. They have all died or moved. I last saw the corner seven years ago. It was late October. Vespucci had sent me. Some leaves and dust were blowing in the air. An ice cream wrapper stuck to my foot. I wondered who could be eating ice cream still. A girl about nineteen smiled when I unstuck it. Tweed skirt and pale blue sweater. Voluptuous. I have since raped her many times. I could have chosen to seduce her, but that would not have been as satisfying. I have named her Melinda, for her great beauty. The first time I was sitting, looking out my window. Since I am on the fourth floor I saw pigeons, wires, rooftops, sky, and in the sky a moving speck. I was thinking, but not very seriously, about masturbation. Not as a release or an excitement, but merely as a possibility, like tying shoelaces, or eating, or studying the calendar. For two years I had looked in the mirror and sorted things out. I don't know exactly why I came to McCoomb Street. To find God? To find myself? Perhaps they are the same. It may be that I have found the devil. I had some idea of removing the intangibles and impedimenta from my life, of working within utterly severe limitations and digging to some core, some truth. This is not the way of my world, which is opening outward to the stars. The magnitude of that endeavor, and the danger, frightens me. What could I find there? I should only lose myself. My inner constellations have at least the redeeming factor that they are nourished by my blood. To be sure, I found myself working in strange ways, but who was I to judge or qualify sincere actions in the service of truth? Truth has risks. I took them. Gladly. My first two years had been hard but rewarding. I was coming to see the pagurian creature who inhabited my skin, who looked out through my eyeballs. Not that I did not have hesitations. There were terrifying holes I dared not descend, let alone look over the rim of. But I was satisfied. I was moving on. I had accomplished something. Melinda knocked. I did not move. I do not know how she found me. She came up behind me and slid her soft white arms over my shoulders. They were not really as milky smooth as I had expected. The fleshy part underneath had a prickly texture. Perhaps she was excited. She had a faint odor of cheap soap. But I was not fussy. I pulled her over the back of the chair and threw her on the floor. I remember she hit her head, and a look of pain and confusion crossed her face. It nearly discouraged me that first time. I am not brutal by nature. At least I don't think I am. I ripped her clothes off and did it. The sex thing. I did not speak to her because I did not want to break the mood. When she picked up her rags and left I noticed the tiny bit of blood on the floor. I left it. Someday, perhaps, my landlady, Mrs. Maldive, would see it and turn purple with jealous rage. It would serve her right. I did not mind the fourth floor. It was the top floor. Outside, my corner of the building looked like a tower. It was rounded, and ended in a turret just above my head. There was no way into the turret, or at least none that I knew. I thought about it often. I don't really like an empty space above me. Oddly, I never wondered about the three floors beneath me. I had one window, facing east, a direction I loathed. West, even north and south, was tolerable. I could, if necessary, endure the ambiguity of northeast or southeast. But east gave me indigestion. It upset my plans. It plagued me. Why not a shade? Because I detest hypocrisy. I could not bear such an obvious evasion. Usually I sat with my back to the window. Except when Melinda came. I liked always to greet her with the back of my head. It also gave her an opportunity for surprises. I trusted her implicitly. Anyway, it was our pattern. I confess, in spite of my efforts, to sentimentality. My room is trapezoidal except for the rounded part near the window. It took me a long time to get used to it. No arrangement of furniture seemed to work. I finally put everything in the middle of the room, facing inward. It is very cozy and gives me a chance to walk in circles around the perimeter. That is my exercise. Exercise is one of my great pleasures, but naturally I have to be careful. Why? I don't really care to say. The furniture is drab but durable. I have four drawers in my dresser. I keep my socks and private things in the top drawer. A few shirts are in the second. The third I leave empty. In the bottom drawer I have odds and ends. My canteen, for example, and some buttons I've collected. On top there is a mirror that moves too easily on its hinges. But I'm glad it's movable. If I tilt it forward I can see my ankles and feet. Sometimes I tilt it back so that I can see just my head, as if it were floating. My mirror is very important to me, though not nearly so much as it used to be. I keep my reading just in front of the mirror, not so close that it will interfere with the movement but quite far from the front. I have reduced my reading to an absolute minimum. I have a telephone book from a small community a thousand miles away. It was not easy to get. I also have an old tide book, but this I do not read unless I am feeling very fit. It brings on fever. I used to have logarithmic tables, but I found I was being sucked into those spaces to the right of the decimals. I like my reading to have an absolute clarity. For that reason I despise the middle initials in the telephone books. I am slowly filling in the names. Do you know any female middle names beginning with "Q" or "X"? I have two covers whose titles are no longer decipherable. I've nailed them to the wall with the gutted ribs showing. Sometimes when I'm walking I run my fingers along the inside. It is an electrifying experience. I have a bed of course. Iron frame and rusty springs. The mattress is lumpy and never seems to be entirely rid of the damp. I have come close to suspecting Mrs. Maldive of deliberately wetting it while I am in the bathroom. In one corner it smells perpetually of old mothballs. Of course it could be something else which to me smells like old mothballs. Maybe there is a dead mouse inside. But I'm being silly. I like the smell very much. When I am unhappy I sleep with my head there. I have made a study of the lumps on both sides of the mattress and arrange myself each night in a new position. Sometimes I avoid all the lumps. That requires me to be quite serpentine. Other times I fit the lumps into my hollows. My hollows are interesting. For example, my lying hollows are different from my standing hollows. Not entirely, naturally. Some overlap. Occasionally I deliberately suffer and allow the lumps to jab my sensitive areas, of which there are several. I have slept so far in 92 different positions on one side of the mattress and in 106 positions on the other side. However, I have not fully explored the possibilities. Perhaps some day I shall have one for each night of the year. Then I might catalog them by date. Mrs. Maldive offered me another mattress 21 months ago and I nearly bit her head off. There has been too much water under the bridge. Perhaps I made a mistake. I am still relatively young. Perhaps the one she was offering me was even lumpier. But I do not trust her. It would not have shocked me too much if the new mattress had closed over me the first night like a *Dionaea muscipula*. I should have been her love-breakfast. The seasons fortunately do not make much difference in the surface of my mattress. I remember at first I was afraid of the inevitable changes. A lump here would shift, a new lump develop there. I had great doubts about the interior consistency. Those fears caused sleepless nights. But I was foolish. The mattress has held up magnificently. To be sure, I am aware of *differences*. I am a realist. But these differences manifest themselves with evolutionary slowness. My mattress is often like some silent and still earth waiting for the hand of God to touch it with life. Sometimes I feel it quickening, but ever so slightly, beneath me, and the feeling is a good one. In the beginning I liked the map metaphor for my mattress. I saw it progressing onward from the early simple maps of Herodotus and Eratosthenes, gradually increasing in scope and complexity to the medieval and the modern. I was quite charmed by the geographical ignorance. It was quaint. I saw change measured by the slow steps of Marco Polo crossing Asian deserts. But I abandoned it early. Already the Roman Empire made me hesitate, and the thought of the Crusades actually distressed me. I realized soon that history was out of the question. It was too much. It was too fast. I should have felt chaos bubbling beneath me. I retreated. The most change I could endure was a million years of drought. Perhaps, if I were pressed, one of the ice ages of the Pleistocene. Since it is a large bed there are also possibilities of a folded mattress. I have not even touched any of these. My future is full. I feel like a squirrel with innumerable tasty nuts tucked away against the cold and ice. Or rather, I did. I shall come to that. Don't trust anything I say. I get carried away. I am deceitful. I cannot master perspective. I cannot assemble properly. I keep forgetting that everything has changed. But has it, really? Has anything changed? In addition to the mattress I have a quilt. The patchwork is faded but dazzling in its variety. It was the quilt that got me started in reading the signs. I originally began with a contemplation of the loose threads—how long, how many whorls, from which patch, their direction, their relation to one another, and so on. Then I discovered a better method, which in turn, by no process of logic, led me to the toilet. Better method of what, you ask? Ah, that is a question to ponder. I warn you, my methodology is unorthodox. I shall trap you into ludicrous assents and affirmations. I am possibly quite mad. But I want you to love me, to know me. I am a jolly fellow. I love animals. I can be quite gentle. I like to laugh. My method of rising never varies. I awaken before dawn, before the sun strikes through the window. I lie there, utterly still, staring out the window until I become infuriated with the inevitability of the rising sun. When I can bear it no longer I leap up and throw off the quilt. And that is the marvel. I am completely calm. I am pacified. I am happy. The quilt never falls the same way. Each day it is cunningly folded anew. Each day it lies in wait for me with new mystery. If I follow a ridge, it disappears into some crevasse, perhaps never to reappear, perhaps, many folds over, to trickle out inconspicuously. The interior is dark, and though many paths lead in I cannot follow without changing the pattern, destroying the integrity. A million throws and each would be different. Do I need libraries? Do I need philosophy? Do I need the world? Here is my *Bible*. By all the infinite possibility surrounding a core of mystery do I see God's incomprehensible but always fascinating purpose unfold. You have twenty questions? Good. Consider them answered. Look to the quilt. Somewhere in the unfolding am I, waiting to be born. *Born*. These, however, are not the readings. No. I still have pagan blood in me. My first few hours in the morning are spent with my quilt. My quilt and I. There is a title for you. Unless, of course, the sun does not rise. Then I pass the morning *under* my quilt. That is quite another matter. Quite. In either case, late in the morning my bowels prompt me elsewhere. I am fortunate in having regular bowels and only one other boarder on my floor. I have never seen him. We share a toilet in the hall. But it is nearer my room than his. He moves his bowels always before I move mine, and then he is gone until evening except on weekends. So the toilet is mine all day if I wish it. I do not. I take only an hour. In that hour I ascertain the state of my health and make, I think, a fair estimate of the condition of the world. I give way a good deal to impulse here, sometimes stripping myself completely, sometimes withholding my faeces, sometimes singing as I unload. But sooner or later it is the same: I shatter the stillness of the toilet water with my turd. It is always a mixture of shock and pleasure, but this is common knowledge. Here, I am afraid you will smile. But you are quite wrong to do so. You are being deceitful, two-faced. You take your defecations as seriously as I do. It is your private little time also. Only you do not talk much about it, except to your doctor. And with him you use formal, cautious terms. Your stool is greenish, you say. Your movement was loose, but not completely loose. You have not evacuated for six days, could he poke his finger for you please. But where is the convulsion of fear that nearly killed you while you were sitting? Do you ever mention that the green is the color of a snail you once saw in a dank alley as a child, that you remember dreaming of that snail for many years, that the puffy softness of that weirdly moving body still haunts you? Where is that glimpse into the abyss, whose edge you forever walk on? You have buried it; it sinks like a stone in your mind's ocean, there to lie with other curious and shadowy objects. You pull up your pants and feel strong again. How simple. A little toilet paper, a flush, and you sit once more on the pinnacle of two thousand years of civilization. What a wondrous world! Perhaps your toilet paper is mono-grammed. Or scented. You do not see your turd as a cor-respondence with another, truer world. Nor do you communicate your pleasure, your wonder, your relief, the myriad subtle thoughts that flash through your mind as you sever yourself from it. No, not even to yourself. You never admit that your comfort is profound, that without that act your day, your love, your success would fall to pieces. Where are your thousand cute, droll, conceited meditations? When you look in the mirror, do you allow yourself to see the proud manufacturer of a healthy turd that very morning? No. It is all vanished. You flush it all away. But aren't you very wrong? Even immoral, in the deepest sense? It is vulgar, you say. I am a noble creature. (Do you think I disagree?) It is crude, coarse, uncivilized. One does not think of shit. One does not talk about shit. Children are quickly hushed. It is no laughing matter. When your child pulls you by the hand to see what he has done, you screw your face. Good, it's done. Like a crocodile, he says, a giant frog, two wolves, and you look embarrassed and flush. Tell me where civilization would be without defecation. Can you see the bloated image as it roams the world? Perhaps it is familiar. You have seen it in your dreams. Are you not a very smug creature? To shit, verb intransitive. But I don't quibble. Make it transitive, if you wish. Conjugate it in the present perfect tense. Give me the first person plural of the future perfect tense (and don't forget "shall"). There, you are smiling. That already is better. Let us join hands. Now you are seeing it, are you not? One of the great processes of history. It is an emblem that has applicability both in science and in art. We shit ourselves out in many ways, and are better off for it. Free yourself of belittling limitations. Do not hide yourself on your toilet. Open your eyes, open your heart, as you open your bowels. There is a new metaphysics awaiting you. I wipe myself carefully and put the folded paper on a small table, which also contains soap, tooth-brushes, and my neighbor's powder and long handled brush. I know he sprinkles himself liberally with the powder because I have smelled the powder in the hall, and when I sit each morning I lift the can once to gauge the loss in weight. Since he does not bathe, he must use it after the toilet. I have had speculations about that, but it is really none of my business. I get up and rearrange my clothes. Then I inhale. Deeply. If I smell nothing at all, I know I am thriving. Not that there is no smell. No. Someone else might be powerfully aware of smell. But if I am not, then I consider that some significant balance between me and my excretion has been struck. However, if I smell something, then I have to decide such things as whether it is more a matter of the upper or lower intestine, the result of nervousness, delay, and so on. Then I look at the thing itself. I make my calculations mainly on the basis of color, size, and number. It is almost a grammatical matter. Any color from dark brown to brown-yellow is good. Black, gray, green, and whitish are bad. No size is too large to be bad. In fact, if it is very large I feel quite pleased because of the implied state of muscular relaxation. The sphincter is a sensitive index. However, I am willing to accept quite small turds also, but not so small as deer dung. And pellets worry me. One morning you would have thought a mouse used the toilet. Likewise I prefer a long healthy strip, and as it is broken up I become more disturbed. All this, I should say, takes me about 35 to 40 minutes. No doubt I could arrive at a conclusion more quickly if I had a formula and knew how to use a computer. But I do the best I can. I am left with about 20 to 25 minutes for a vision of everything outside me. For this I use the handle of the brush. I realize it is remiss, but there is no other stick around. I try never to get more than two inches of it wet. My neighbor, as I mentioned, never bathes, so the brush is never wet except from my use. He does, however, use the brush because the bristles are worn and falling out. Perhaps he gives himself a dry brush or uses it to apply his powder. I don't know. I don't wish to complicate my life more than necessary. I'm sometimes terribly afraid my use of his brush will lead to the very complications I wish to avoid. I do dry it thoroughly, but of course the damp cannot be disguised. What I do is stir the water in the bowl vigorously 36½ times. The swirl is always different. I have no incantations, though sometimes I hum. I cannot have interruptions. If I lose count I must start over. Even if my neighbor were to come in, he would have to wait until I finished the requisite number of stirs. And what would I say to him? It is an idiotic situation to imagine, is it not? I really have no suitable answer. The occasion will have to supply it. Fate, unfortunately, is full of such exigencies. It is mainly in the vortex that I see things, although the way the turds come to rest is often revealing. For example, sometimes they sink, sometimes they float, sometimes some sink and some float. Occasionally, some stick to the sides, left high and dry when the swirl subsides. The final configurations are infinite. Ridiculous, you say? Why is it more ridiculous than any other method of diagnosis or prognosis? My food, after all, comes from the world at large, and I share with the rest of humanity my organs, my flesh, my blood. Do you not recognize connections when you see them? You read your newspaper; I shall stick to my toilet bowl. The old readers of entrails knew what they were doing. One truth is as good as another, and sometimes better. I go through this procedure six or seven times, and then, after wiping the brush clean and depositing my soiled papers, flush. I have had a run of luck until just recently and my outlook was optimistic. Two winters ago I had digestive troubles for several days. I believe I came close to suicide after reading the signs. They were black days. I realize there are many variables I do not take into account. For example, the season or the number of hours I have slept or the water levels in the reservoirs. What effect would a different toilet bowl have? What if I used *three* inches of the brush? What about density? Would it be playing fair to use laxatives or suppositories? What if my neighbor changed his habits? Well, what can I say but that I feel I have evolved a reasonable method for my readings. I am not about to add weights and measures. There is a point beyond which science calculates the meaningless. One, after all, must make *some* kind of leap in this life. I also have two chairs. One is quite firm and straight. I do my eating and correspondence on it. (I have had no correspondence yet but do write notes to myself, sometimes very surprising notes. I do not recognize myself in them.) The other is a parlor chair. It is lopsided and creaky. I think it conceals insect kingdoms, but they must be very discreet. I never see them. I am saving them for my old age. I relax in it and meditate. On what? Well, for example, am I myself or the shadow of myself, and the existential ramifications of either answer. Neat, is it not? What would be the benefit of being able to feel my liver function? (There is philosophy here.) What has one head, five legs, and no holes? It is also the chair in which I greet Melinda. Ah, Melinda. She has aged

97

little in all these years. In spite of her brutal home life. Her father beats her. I never know how to distinguish his bruises from mine. She is a patient and faithful girl. Sometimes I think I am undeserving. I feel that I do not have enough to offer, that our relationship is lacking in tender moments, that we do not have true rapport. But when I hear her sliding up behind me, feel the touch of her fleshy arms, hear the thud and see the terrified look in her eyes, I know it is all right. Passion spans all barriers. In love we are all united. I have plans for her, but the time is not ripe. We must get to know each other better. Only then can I ask her, perhaps, to share my life. I long to have her read the signs with me. Together we shall go so much further. And then, too, I feel she might add just that small touch of color, of gaiety, that my life needs to be complete. Not that I am without color. I have a small hexagonal table. I would have preferred a circle, but this suffices. It is a brownish color and very shiny. One leg is shorter than the others, but I have compensated for that by finding a warped floor board. I put the short leg on the warp and everything is shipshape. It has a small drawer with a screw in it, but I have not yet discovered where the screw goes. But I will. Almost exactly in the middle is a splotch of green paint. It is worn and faded, but clearly green. It must have been dropped by a painter while painting. Nothing in my room is green so it is something of a puzzle. Perhaps another room. But that is too easy. Why move such an insignificant piece of furniture? I pride myself that I know Mrs. Maldive well enough to say she would not under any circumstances transpose furniture. Her occupations are not so obvious. Perhaps many years ago the walls were green. Now they are wall-papered. White but covered with soot. They are really gray. I began peeling one day to find the green. But under the gray I found another gray. And under that still another. And then another. At that point it was difficult to peel further without removing larger strips, so I just scratched through with the screw in the drawer to the next surface. It was a brilliant red! At first I thought the wall was bleeding and during one horrified instant saw myself enclosed in walls through which blood circulated. Pure fantasy, of course. But there is my color. I have the green splotch and the scratch of red. It is enough. I dread the thought of those red walls buried all around me. There is something oriental about them. Sometimes I feel on the verge of insane indulgence. What would happen if I stripped all the walls down to the red? A very pretty question. I am grateful for the protecting layers of gray. The green splotch is not nearly so frightening. It reminds me often of my mother. Between four and six in the afternoon, more in the autumn than in other seasons, the splotch looks exactly like my mother after supper. She had a contented look crossed by disapproval of her contentment. That was when she was most likely to snap at me. To protect myself I tried to look sick and unhappy after supper. Sometimes I pretended to vomit. Then she would stroke my head in the parlor and be nice. But can that really be my mother? Was I reduced to such extremities? Was she not a sweeter creature? I am slightly deranged at the moment. Forgive me. I cannot remember properly. I cannot connect. She was an unhappy woman, I think. Father never spoke after supper. On the stroke of nine he marched double time to bed. Mother followed at nine-thirty. For some odd reason I was allowed to stay up as late as I liked. It was as if I did not belong to the family. Those hours after nine-thirty were happy and interesting hours for me. I could twiddle my thumbs in complete enjoyment until midnight. I knew every sound, from the dripping in the sink to the creaks in the floor, intimately. It was my world, my very own. The green splotch brings it all back. But that is only four to six in the autumn. Other times I see animals or things or secrets. The secrets are the best. I remember one rainy spring morning I glanced almost accidentally at the splotch. It was turning, at first slowly, then more rapidly. Finally there was a hole in the middle and a finger came out. Then I heard a voice saying, "You. You. You. You." The finger receded, the voice faded, and the whirling stopped. I was trembling with joy. That was one of the secrets. Of course a lot depended on how I approached the table, from what direction and height. It was a stupendous discovery one day when I crawled up to the table, my eye level with the surface. At first I saw nothing. Then a green line. As I got closer, my eyes naturally wavered, as did my whole body. I am not a precision machine. And accordingly my perspective changed too. It was a moving experience. Not only did I see small bumps and ripples where formerly I had seen flat, but the thousands of imperceptible changes in my movement, and in my respiration, gave me the sensation of moving into a continent of green. I got dizzy, probably with excitement, and had to stop. Eventually I learned to steady myself and enter the green in earnest. They were swash-buckling times. So much for my furniture. There are some minor things. There is a chamber pot, but I have only recently used it in seven years. It is cracked anyway. I don't think it was originally a chamber pot, but what it was I can't imagine. I have a glass coaster which was once used under the leg of a bed and which Mrs. Maldive now offers as an ashtray. She knows I do not smoke. In fact, it was after she discovered I did not smoke that she brought the coaster. Our relations have been fraught with mischief and misunderstanding from the beginning. Once she did not replace my only bulb for two weeks. I was prey to a million fears while I lived in darkness. Possibly I screamed once or twice. If I did, I am sure she laughed. And she contaminates my food with dish water and roach poison. I don't know what she wants. (I'm lying, of course.) It infuriates me that she persists in her smoking joke. Once a week she leaves a book of matches outside my door, but all the heads have been cut off. My window has a shade. I mentioned that. I never pull it. I might not wake for days. My slippers are old but durable. Some kind of lizard skin. I have three shirts which I launder myself, two pairs of pants, and one sweater, fairly motheaten but warm. I used to have a fly swatter, but I threw it out the window one day. Mrs. Maldive has cunningly never admitted that she found it. I can see her laughing in her kitchen, a fly swatter in each hand, performing some crude hippopotamic dance as she executes flies. The dance of the two fly swatters. She probably puts the flies in my food. Sometimes I deliberately leave a crumb on my plate. I want her to know that if I choose I can recognize the foul things she puts in my meals. My shoes are excellent. I tread softly and uniformly. I keep them well aired. I do not use laces because they would wear out too quickly and erode the shoes. By keeping my feet tensed I can keep the shoes on my feet quite well. That, I think, covers my room. The hall outside is dim. My landlady uses a fifteen watt bulb. There are four doors, my door, my neighbor's, the bathroom, and one leading to a closet. I do not know what Mrs. Maldive keeps there. I often hear her rummaging. I suspect there is a way up to the turret above me. I have spent whole days putting on an act because I was certain she was there. I have a marvelous seal act. I crouch on my little table and slap my hands together while bobbing my head and barking. I also have a mole act and a snake act. I can see that I had better tell you about Mrs. Maldive.

Mrs. Maldive, I

NICE MAN FRESH FELLA TICKEL BRESTIE CUTE DEVIL WINK IN
wild eye kid I having crazy cunti big fun juice I going hot BAZOOM
so HE dont care he DRUNK all time I playing round regular new
fella got sexi go slam in nose me *damn* (!)!

not hoping he door yet get I mad I giving room cheap nasty fella he
no play with me I show him kick in ass good

where little girl I sad for kill him little bastit he no good & write no
more & why he tease me not so bad got shape in still know wiggle
ass bet I rolling good in hay get going

pluck pluck pluck chick in kitchen get him soon he bite we laugh in
pluck I cook him good

prair mother virgin give me hot fuck

he not play ball I mad & giving me come on wink eye tickel me no
more I smelling rat in skunk I fixing good his wagon hah hah

got spy spot he take it out big stick cock I crazy going kill him soon
she sweet little baby cry I girl oh where she is that little baby kill this
bastit cheat me not any damn big fool I guess

hahahahahahahahahahahahahahahahahahahahahahahahaha
hahahahahahahahahahahahahahahahahahahahahahahahahaha
hahahahaha

I keeping food his mout & starve hungri good show bastit

I getting all wet spy hole breaking roof he shoot me everytime &
why he dont vite me HE dont know he DRUNK all time I nice I give
him good I ready going all time now sweat he tease me bad I killing
him bastit breaking leg & (and) sit him fart I prair all time he come

he crazy bastit

why I live so rotten damn I good girl nobody slap on back & where
little blondi cry so hard I give him chance he shit all time dont look
me even wink me all doll up in stick in powder like hotdog movie girl

good ol day got fuck anyway prair mother marry

hahahahahahahahahahahahahahahahahahahahahahaha!!!!!!!!!!???
????!!!!!!!!!! throw rag in toilette make him mess

meet crazy girl she grabbing ass is sweet but who she doing why I
say huh

she church girl big blondi where my baby we do nasti thing I like he
son of bich bastit

god damn I dirty thing no prair no good I like my blondi kill me good
I show him crazy bastit like queer he never write my baby where is I
got mixed don't!?!?!?!?!?!

he dont never coming hermit coon crazy is like coocoo birdi lock my
door I smarter fix his wagon catch smash I get him all me ready in
every minute now she kill me blondi why she gone I luve her little
baby getting me is mad I blowing up got sliver bastit kill him

hahahahahahahahahahahahahahahahahahahahahahahahaha
hahahahahahahahahahahahahahahahhheeheeheeheeheeheehee
heeheeheeheeheeheeheehaheehaheehaheehaheehahahahahaha
heeheeheehee he dont play me get away

eat like pig I hungry everytime

albem show me pretty crying all time & why they go he drunk she crazy girl I kill him bastid where my blondi baby now

bandon me every shit bastit I roll in fat like pig I killing self I so miserate

I nut like fruiti crazy loon I give him big snap I pull I catch I eat him down he think he smart I get him good

what for I good girl I prair I stink whole damn big stink it everywhere I give big fart haha

I get me dog I get me pussy cat I kill him stupit bastit

me mad me mad me mad me mad me mad me mad me mad me mad me mad me mad bang bang bang bang bang bonk bonk bonk bonk bonk bonk rip rip rip rip rrrrrrrrrrrrrrrrrrrrr me teeth me sharp me bite me kill me snapping bone me crush me step on head me growl me squashing good me twist me squeezing blood I drink me tearing hart I smash in head I step on brain I make in soup I shit on step I throw in toilette he don't get way he stick it cunti blondi girl he stead me crook he queer I kill him stupit bastit to I smash him hole I throw it down she stink oh marry why you dont here my prair

I get him good

he scare

ha ha ha ha ha ha ha ha ha ha ha ha ha ha ha ha ha ha ha ha

me

Mrs. Maldive, II

SHE WAS LYING ON TOP OF ME, PANTING LIKE SOME EXPIRING beast of the late Mesozoic, a rancid lust stirring her into fetid unction beneath the layers of fat. I could feel the clogged canals floating out the debris of five thousand nights. I could hear her organs sloshing, riding the crest of her unleashed sensuality. I was grateful for the ceiling. It was all that kept me from being inundated. I could not have withstood her. I could not have resisted her crushing embrace and those slashing teeth. And I brought it all on myself. I misjudged her. Grotesquely. *I did not know her.* After Melinda smiled I walked to the sixth house on McCoomb Street. I did not know then why. I rather fancied its castlelike appearance. The windows were dirty. Pigeons littered the ledges. The grass was uncut. The house had stopped living. Actually, it was waiting. Perhaps I saw myself in the guise of a prince who would kiss it back to strength and beauty. Mrs. Maldive herself answered my knock. She was a revelation to me. Her bulk was enormous. She was only five feet but weighed at least three hundred pounds. My impression was not immediately of fatness, however, but of power. She looked as if she had built the house of flesh she lived in. She had on one of those cheap but cheerful kitchen dresses with no sleeves. Her head was small in proportion, with small blue eyes and red ears, a wide flat nose, and a small mouth. Her hair was frizzy. When I asked her whether she had a room she smiled, and I saw that she had many large teeth and a cavernous interior. Once past her lips, which were thin and hard, one was sure of a quick death. She was monstrous, but my reaction was, oddly, one of surprise rather than shock. She uttered something in a language closer to passionate noise than discourse, and I sensed that I had reached some destination, some end. I shrugged and held out my hands in appeasement, and in so doing brushed lightly her left nipple. Her pealike eyes bulged and she showed me all her teeth, which I now saw went in all directions and could probably chew food in a hundred different ways. She pushed out her lower lip with a very fluffy tongue and stepped back. I followed, and the door shut with finality. In the dark I felt her stubby fingers wiggle me. I was petrified. She had so totally misconstrued my gesture. To my immense relief, we soon went up several flights of stairs. My eyes were level with her elephantine buttocks, and in spite of my fear I was impressed. I looked around the room quickly, came back to the door where she was standing with her tongue lolling seductively over her lip, and slammed it in her face. I have often wondered how long it took her to pull her tongue in and what it tasted like. It was not a pretty tongue. I like pink, pointy tongues. Hers was really fluffy, that is, hairy. White hairy. Microbes must have scooted in and out of it like fish on a coral reef. I listened but heard nothing. She must have smelled me there, for she never moved. Later I heard her for the first time rummaging in the hall closet. God knows what she kept there. Probably old bones and dirty memories. I thought nothing of it for nearly a year. One day in late summer I noticed the ceiling sagging. It had over the months become discolored in a certain area, and I fancied the discoloration was about the size of a basking walrus. Of course it was Mrs. Maldive. She had access to my turret through her closet. It was down the hall, to be sure, but she could easily crawl or wriggle the thirty or so feet under the eaves. It must have taken her bulk an hour each way. And the slivers! I can see her slow wet progress, punctuated by the pricks of a rotten floor, and pity her for her gargantuan lust. She mortified her flesh in the service of the devil. Whether she did this naked or not I never discovered. In fact we never broached the subject. But I am convinced that at regular intervals she made the obscene pilgrimage and lay above my ceiling like a grotesque succubus spying on me. I could feel the suction, feel myself rising off the floor, crashing through the ceiling to satisfy her mammoth thirst. Helpless among her nightmare folds, at the mercy of pre-Cambrian secretions and steely purpose. What god here practiced his cancerous whim, I wondered. What monstrous end was here being served? Half paralyzed with the stupendous fatality of it all, I decided to fight back. I made a show of passion, but never letting on that I guessed her oily proximity. I unzipped and took out my identity and went through military formations. I always ended up by saluting the flag and firing salvos. God, how the ceiling creaked and heaved. But it held. It held. And later there would be rummaging again in the closet, hot breath on my door, and silence. It was not an ideal situation. If I had not had Melinda I might not have borne it. She was a balm. She lightened my days. I was fortunate that Mrs. Maldive never saw me with her. She would have consumed us both in the budding of our love. Once we had ordered our respective passions we were able to relate on a civilized plane, though I was always aware of an undercurrent of hostility and resentment, and there were always little incidents. For example, at one point she began to leave her menstrual napkins in my toilet bowl. I knew that if I flushed them the toilet would overflow. At first I plucked them out and put them in the trash basket. Once I just flung them down the stairs, but that did not give me satisfaction. Finally I came upon the perfect solution. I incorporated them into my readings and when finished did not flush the toilet. What my neighbor did with it all when he came home at night I don't know. He must have learned quickly which part he could flush and which not. I never heard anything about it. Perhaps he saw everything as a coy overture from his landlady. It doesn't really matter. Mrs. Maldive had been quite blocked. True, for six or so days a month we three were bound up in an uncomfortable if intricate relationship. I did not mind myself because it did add something to the readings. No doubt Mrs. Maldive wanted to impress me with her fertility. But I was not impressed. It could have been chicken blood. It could have been anything. I have good reason to believe that my neighbor ultimately *was* impressed, but of that later. Let me try to tell everything as I experienced it. Another of Mrs. Maldive's stunts occurred in my eighteenth month. I was well into my routine. My readings had been most favorable for several weeks. I consequently entered the bathroom and dropped my pants each morning with great assurance. One morning I had done just so and, not having any games, was well into my stool when I noticed Mrs. Maldive in the bathtub. She was stark naked and smoking a cigarette in a long bejeweled holder. I immediately cut my stool and stood up. Then I sat down again and wiped myself. I was confused. She said nothing. Indeed her face was expressionless. She just stared with her pea eyes at me. She had on globs of rouge and lipstick, and I believe she had powdered her hair, probably a sudden patriotic inspiration engendered by memories of George Washington. I don't know what she expected. There could hardly have been room for me in the tub even if I had seen the occasion as an opportunity. My strongest memory is that her nipples were different colors, although that might have been the lighting. I half expected her to break out into a German love song, but she did not. She looked like a bewildered beached manatee, and had there been an estuary nearby I would have rolled her down to it. I felt a little ashamed and, oddly, touched. It was, after all, an affectionate gesture, however badly staged. I zipped up and left without a word. Later, when I returned, she was gone. I tried to finish my movement, but I had become constipated. My system had received a shock. I remained constipated for several days, and when I got over it I had one of the most depressing readings I had ever had. All that I owe to Mrs. Maldive. She did, however, have her better moments. I must grant her that. Usually I have my meals in my room. Because I am on the fourth floor, I have agreed to have my breakfast and lunch together. It is a meager meal, and I am starved most of the day. Mrs. Maldive knows I am at her mercy in many ways. When she is in one of her moods I get crackers and water. Sometimes I go to bed without supper. Usually at breakfast I get a cold fried egg, a piece of toast, and tea. I insist on my tea. Dinner is always at five. Mrs. Maldive serves three or four standard meals. They never vary. Mondays it is stew. Tuesdays it is day old stew with water added. Wednesdays it is chopped meat, either square or round, parboiled potatoes, and a green. Thursdays the same, with the potatoes mashed or browned in a greasy pan. Fridays it is fish and cooked tomatoes. Saturdays it is soup and croquettes, both made up from all the leftovers of the week. What is left of the soup becomes next week's gravy, so that each week has something of the previous week's menu. In fact, each meal has something of all past meals in it, which makes for an interesting digestive, even historical, continuity. Whether or not she starts fresh each year I don't know. Occasionally, when she has accidentally cooked a tasty meal, I can still taste it in the gravy weeks later, and it is a sweet compensation for the drabness of the meal it embellishes. In the beginning I allowed her to bring the meal directly into my room, but she too often stayed to watch me eat. I never knew whether I was eating or being eaten. Even when she did not stay, a glimpse of her eyes and teeth was enough to ruin the readings next day. I felt constantly threatened. I finally prevailed upon her to leave the tray outside my door. I was engaged in serious work. Interruption would be fatal. If I were free, I would leave the door open. Her feeble mind grasped at that straw. Of course the door was never open. She did not realize whose hand was upon the straw. In her cunning she would linger by the door, sometimes for hours. But I was equal to her cunning. I waited. The food, after such waits, was usually solidified into the gravy that covered it, but I did not mind. It was rather like a nutritious mucous, and I ate with perverse joy. Sometimes she rushed into her closet, but I knew her intention. Well before she squirmed onto her outline on the ceiling I had finished the meal and frustrated her anger for variety. Had there been no ceiling at such moments, I am sure she would have ripped me to pieces. I had to keep my door bolted at all times. I came to that decision after two years. My timing was fortunate. Several days after I first bolted my door I saw the knob turn. There was never a knock, never a sound. After a while I got used to it. Since I am a person of profound habit, there was no danger of accident. I got pleasure out of my infallibility in this area. My greatest periods of vulnerability were my trips to the toilet. For some reason, she never chose those times to attack. My bowels were respected. Nevertheless I reduced my trips to a minimum. I regulated my bladder, I increased its capacity. I even repaired the chamber pot for emergencies during the night. Sometimes I could hear her sleeping outside my door, like some dragon of dream. I was able to know something of her malign plots against my person by a study of my dinner trays. She revealed her simple nature often in the arrangement of food. If everything was arranged too precisely, no item touching another, the amounts sufficient, the gravy spread uniformly—I was prepared for the utmost cunning of which she was capable. I did not mind because I knew she would have method in whatever she did. I could combat that. What was far worse was chaos. Everything thrown together, the gravy spilling off the plate, the amounts almost indistinguishable, and when distinguishable then disproportionate. That meant she had gone over the edge. I had driven her too far. Her brontosauric lust had pushed her into a madness which could have no method. Then I was frightened. I used my chamber pot until it overflowed. I had no clear notion of what she was capable. In fact, only once did I get even a glimpse, and that reinforced my belief that safety at such times lay in virtual self-imprisonment. One evening Mrs. Maldive had put my tray down and gone away immediately. I was at once suspicious. I listened at the door for twenty minutes and heard nothing. When I opened it, I looked up and down the hall and up at the ceiling. I half expected to see her hanging there like a huge, small-eyed spider ready to drop on some intestinal cord and devour me. She was not there. The tray, I noticed, was slightly elevated. My mind worked furiously. I dared not put my fingers under it. I knew that my most normal actions would betray me, plunge me into horror. After a few moments I picked up the spoon and began edging it off whatever was beneath it. That was foolish. She was capable even of explosive devices where her lust was concerned. She would have glutted herself on my mutilated body without remorse. Nor would I have been surprised, as I moved the tray, to see her eyes peering up at me. Say that I am a fool, but nothing was beyond her at such moments. She had an evil genius. Suddenly, where my left hand would have grasped the tray, there was a loud snap. I saw the cracked tray before I saw the stained metal bar of an enormous rat trap which had cracked it. And no sooner did I see the bar than the tray began scuttling down the hall like a mechanical crab, pulled by a thick umbilical cord which had been slyly tucked against the wall.

As the tray went over the precipice, throwing off its food with abandon, I saw what my fate was to have been, I saw the thick, powerful arms below, the waiting mouth with its slashing teeth like some devouring Moloch, and the bottomless flesh. I shuddered and closed the door against a rage I could already smell. It was only later, when I had calmed myself, that I began to think about the size of the rat trap. Could there possibly be rats so large? And in this house? It was beyond belief. But if not the rats, then it was Mrs. Maldive's own diabolic invention. And I was to be its first victim. Or was I? That doubt eventually led me to a totally new evaluation of Mrs. Maldive. The bar had been distinctly stained! However, I did say she had her better moments. The first dinner of every week we shared like an old married couple. In all my seven years this had never varied. For a reason I shall probably never know, on Sundays Mrs. Maldive relented. Perhaps she went to a religious service which put her in a gentler frame of mind or prompted her to dwell on other worlds, other matters. I don't know. She went no further than to have her last week's underwear drying on a little line by the sink. I easily forgave her that. I came down to the kitchen midafternoon. She would always be sitting at the table, which was set for two. We did not really speak. She opened her mouth and let out something like "Oheeeeyrrr" and I grumbled something suitable back. Then she would go to the cellar door, behind which a chicken had been hanging upside down overnight. She twisted the neck three or four times quickly and then sat down opposite me with the limp body in her lap. Then for forty minutes or so we would pluck feathers out of the still warm body, she giggling all the while as if they were her pubic hairs. Silly, but to tell the truth I rather enjoyed it. It was all very human. It was family. She cooked a good chicken. Her stuffing was superb. Naturally we left nothing but the bones. After storebought blueberry pie and two cups of coffee I helped her clean up. Then we listened to the radio. We were both fond of "The Green Hornet." When darkness fell I could sense the barriers coming down by the spittle at the corners of her mouth as we smirked and grunted at each other. I escaped the first time she turned her back to me. As I raced up the stairs to my room I always heard her plaintive cry, "Oheeeeyrrr," and felt a twinge of shame. But when I heard her puffing up after me, her curses asphyxiated from the exertion, it vanished, and its place was taken by fright. Sunday nights especially did she spend sleeping outside my door. In the morning I could feel the dampness where she had sweated and drooled. And sometimes her breath whistled under the door at night like the cry of some far off bird. I think she must have slept well. One night, to be sure, I was awakened by a horrible crashing. I got the taste of vomit in my mouth as someone hurled himself again and again against my door with sickening thuds. Oddly, my greatest fear during those moments was that it would all happen in the dark. But my door was the door of a castle, and the battered body finally crawled away. I was anxious to get a glimpse of her next day to see if she was bruised, but I could make nothing out through my keyhole. She laid low for some time after that, and I became quite relaxed. I did not realize that she was at that very time preparing a most cruel dilemma for me. But that was not to reveal itself for many, many months, and I used my greater sense of freedom to indulge myself with Melinda. One more incident seems significant, though I cannot explain how or why. It was during one of my periods of deep anxiety. It was night, and it was silent. Outside the wind rustled fallen leaves gently. Autumn had retreated briefly to summer. I lay on my bed, my mind dormant, my body relaxed. I had been listening to it before I realized I heard it. A voice, a soft and sweet voice in the hall, singing a beautiful song about a child and the sea. It was unbearably beautiful. Tears came to my eyes. I got up and walked to the door, fumbling with the bolt. I had to find that voice, touch it, curl up before it and sleep, sleep so peacefully and deeply that it would be like rebirth. And then I smelled her. The bolt was nearly open, and I smelled her, felt the wall of flesh pressing against the door, waiting for release, waiting to destroy me. I hardly had the strength to push the bolt back. I could not breathe. I staggered to the bed and collapsed into a night of nightmare. In the morning, when I awoke, I remembered the voice and the song. I cried. I wished desperately for Melinda to come. And, true to my heart as she always was, she came.

Melinda, I

FORNICATE: "HAVING AN ARCHED, OR VAULTED FORM; ALSO,
having fornices."????

*   *   *   *

True beauty is a love
Blessed from heaven above
When you're breathing near me
I hope that you can hear me
Saying
True beauty is a love
Blessed from heaven above
                    (Repeat)

*   *   *   *

We'll die together
Among the heather
Fragrance in the air
We'll lie together
In every weather
Our love so rare

Your lips aglow
We've got to go
God calls all to rest
I'll kiss you so
That you'll always know
Your lips were the best

In death we'll embrace
Love is our grace
In earth we'll each other hold
Worms cannot eat
Our love can't be beat
We'll never, never grow cold

I adore the Wee Winkles! (and the Wee Willies!!)

*   *   *   *

"A true lover's lips are always poised to kiss."

*   *   *   *

Daddy smacked me on my bare bottom again today. I didn't do anything. I just looked at him. He has such a big hand. Why does he have me take *everything* off? I've found my method!

*   *   *   *

When you looked at me	(Gregory P.)
My heart stumbled	(avalanche)
When you held my hand	(Gregory P.)
My virtue crumbled	(Daddy)
What can a girl do	(hungry, french fries and ketchup)
When your beard rubs her cheek	(pussy cat)
But let you hold her close	(Gregory P.)
Because she is weak	(dish rag)
You led me to sin	(Daddy spank)
I fell all the way	(Daddy spank)
I'm only a girl	(cookie jar)
What can I say	(ocean, thunder, stars)

*　　*　　*　　*

And right across his lap! "If your heart aches, your eyes will show the pain." (He *lingers!*)

*　　*　　*　　*

I've got to get more cleavage. When Gail La Flame pulls out the rose and throws it to her audience they just die! I wonder what perfume she uses. FORNICES: "anatomical arches or folds."???

*　　*　　*　　*

Sing a hucka bucka
Sing a hucka bucka
I gotta lot a lucka
Cause I got you!

Play the hucka bucka
Play the hucka bucka
I like a lotta lucka
When I got you!

Give me hucka bucka
Give me hucka bucka
I need a lotta lucka
When I'm with you!

*　　*　　*　　*

J.G. said I had more bounce to the ounce than anyone he knew. Bombs away!

*　　*　　*　　*

"If your heart is in it, so is God." ARCH: "Cleverly sly and alert;

playfully saucy."???

*   *   *   *

Oh, Daddy, Daddy!

*   *   *   *

Your mother was a beauty rose
She glowed from morn to night
Whene'er she walked there went with her
The glory that was light

But you her bud are just as bright
A lily in the lake
Whenever I do look at you
I feel my heart will break

I wish I were that frog that sits
Upon your lovely lip
But I shall leave you still and white
Your loveliness I'd rip

(Echo chamber)
Pale lily on the lake
I'd die for your sake
Pale lily all alone
Be the wind my moan
(Waves crash on shore, song of sea-gulls)
        (Repeat)

*   *   *   *

Genivieve La Fresca (Sandra Herskowitz) is coming to town! (I read
that she dips her fingernails in blood. When people hear her they
can't take their eyes off her hands. She's had four husbands!

116

Including Jimmie Jukalote who I think is *cute*) ANATOMICAL:
"adj."?????

*   *   *   *

Daddy did it again and a funny thing happened. I was *very*
embarrassed. He just hit me all the harder. Wow! (Wowie!)

*   *   *   *

Do you like your old Daddio
Do you like your old Pa
He's a swell old guy
You could never buy

So give him lots a kissa, kissa
Give him lots of love
He's that one in a million
And you're his dove

Do you like your grand old fella
Do you like your teddy bear
He's cream of the crop
Just keep him on top

And give him lots a kissa, kissa
Give him lots a love
He's that one in a zillion
And you're his turtle dove

"True love is the gift of passion. Love lives in fire." (!!) Amen!

*   *   *   *

Mama's sick. I can do cute things with my tongue. Jimmy H. (Dink)
wets his pants when he's with me. I have lamé panties. Jimmy calls

117

it a golden crotch. (He wants to crotchet!) I only let him touch it.

* * * *

"F——!" (uck)!!!

* * * *

Dress: skin tight, silver sequins. V-neck, V-bottom. Show rear end
a lot (Good feature). Tickle nipples with fan (I pop). Then:

I'm a-flame with love	(hot oven)
I am burning with desire	(Joan of Arc)
Don't dare to touch me	(iceberg)
I'm an electric wire	(electric chair)

I will shock you with love	(Pull the switch)
Let me heat you up tight	(Gregory P.)
Just plug me in the socket	(Daddy spank)
We'll go off like a rocket	(Whoosh!)

In our trip through the stars	(Look up, wide eyes, God looking)
We'll kiss soft and sweet	(pussy cat)
Our love will consume us	(bonfire)
From heat to our feet	(Daddy spank)

So yield to my love	(Gregory P.)
I am blazing away	(nude on Times Square)
Give me your passion	(Gregory P.)
And let come what may!	(Whoosh! Wiggle. Finger. Daddy spank)

Men like women who can make their mouths round and look either
thoughtful or surprised. Men like a girl to smell nice. If a girl stinks
they don't think they're doing anything special. Men are cute. Men
are funny. Down there. It's a big thing with them. (I got very bold

with Dink. I thought he'd die! Umm! Yum!) Mama's still sick. Men like nothing better than to be treated like babies with big ------. Ooops! Flunked everything at school except gym. Who cares? Regalia Columbine never finished sixth grade. And she knows how to swing it. Hey, hey! Screw them all! Met a gorgeous creature. This is it. I'm on my way. *I know it.*

*   *   *   *

"Fate is in the bowels. When you feel it you move."

*   *   *   *

"Confucius say: If ass stuck on mountain, c--- stuck too."

*   *   *   *

"Confucius say: Finger in nose better than finger in ass."

*   *   *   *

Oh, *Daddy!*

Melinda, II

AH, MELINDA! A BARE NINETEEN WHEN I MET HER. HOW SHALL I describe her? A blonde goddess? A ripe fruit? The breath of love? All would be inadequate. When she smiled at me on the corner of McCoomb Street I had no idea that suddenly, two years later, she would glide into my room and surrender herself to me. Yet that is not entirely true. There was, when her eyes crossed mine, a flicker of recognition, of understanding, so quick that it disappeared before I could reflect on it. There were many mysteries to Melinda which I never penetrated. Not the least was why she had waited two years to declare herself. She has given me reasons, but I have not yet the courage to credit them. The time, however, was not wasted. In a way, I prepared myself for her. As I said, during those years I spent much of my time before the mirror sorting things out. The mirror is a great instrument. Few of us realize how great. It is the means of great revelation and terrible truth. I could never finish learning from it. For example, I learned that if I held my mouth in a certain way I could see all of my teeth, absolutely all of them. What is that, you say? Before you ask the question, place yourself before a mirror and contort yourself until you can see all your teeth. Then look into your eyes. I do not believe you will ask the question again. Of course I did not begin with such complicated movements. The first three months I merely looked at myself with whatever expression I happened to have. At first I laughed a lot. I was self-conscious and ashamed of such naked looking. I felt guilty about the pleasure I permitted myself to feel. It was an indulgence, a vanity I ought not to permit. But when I saw all this reflected in the mirror my laughter became grotesque. My face stiffened and I had to turn away for relief from a deceit which was so glaring. At such moments I felt a twinge of the revulsion that I was later to expose more fully; but I dismissed it from my mind quickly. I became angry with myself. What right had I to despise myself so? Why could I not love myself with sincerity and joy? Why could I not love myself in a simple, unaffected way? It was not an easy task to destroy the cringing modesty which masked vanity which masked guilt. But at last I did. I purified myself by fire and was able to look at myself with unadorned curiosity, with liking and respect, with suckling pleasure that tingled my genitals. I saw myself for the first time. And what did I see? I saw a round face with pores visible at twenty feet. My eyes were large and close together. Their color was a nondescript gray. There were three furrows between them, below which the bridge of my nose started from the flat and eased downward in a ski slope that was rimmed on either side by large ovular nostrils which I could see into easily. The hairs in my nose, which I cultivated, invariably had dried mucous which I was forever scraping away with great pleasure. My upper lip was thin and long, the lower loose, fat, and short. The chin receded into the neck. Higher there were small white ears, and directly across, my best feature, sensually curved, bushy eyebrows. My hair was thinning, but evenly and underneath. Occasionally strips of scalp showed when my hair stuck together from sebaceous secretions. I can claim only fair teeth, small, regular, and speckled here and there with black. I had enormous pointed eye-teeth which compensated for my wet baby smile. My beard was slow-growing and thin. When I let it grow a little I fancied I looked like a young rabbi. I did not come to this all at once. No. That would have been impossible. I concentrated on one feature at a time in the beginning. For example, my skin. In a week's time I had ascertained that my pores were not perfectly round, that some were larger than others, that about five percent of them at any given time were erupting into pimples and blackheads. I discovered that the skin on my nose had the most pus when squeezed and that the insides of my ears were constantly scaling. Or take my eyebrows. If I looked at them long enough I seemed bestial. Any human vestiges disappeared. They were funny, odd, crude, coarse, primitive, savage. By concentrating on my eyebrows I learned to wiggle my ears and developed a convincing guttural grunt. And my eyes. Sometimes looking at those delicate liquid orbs floating in a skull made me shudder. What kind of strange creature was this? What tortuous evolution made me? I felt not only a stranger to myself but also a stranger to the creature I was. Where was *I* in all this? How could I place myself? A lemur would have been more familiar. You wonder that I was able to get pleasure from all this? Well, I was. As I felt the birth of honesty I came to love myself. To end hypocrisy all we need do is hold up a mirror. One cannot lie to his own image. Something shows, something gives the lie away. Few people, for example, can make love in front of a mirror. So it was with me. I shed my masks and learned to look at and love what I was. Perhaps I should have stopped there. I don't know. I had nothing to guide me. I was proceeding at that time on the untenable premise that there was only good in me, that the evil was nothing but crusty adhesion of time and society which exposure would scrape off. And I had learned so much about myself in three months. I was romantic. I could spend six hours in front of my mirror in utter fascination. I was a thousand people, and never bored. I was sensitive to the slightest change of expression. The permutations of expression between eyes, nose, and mouth were infinite. It was the visible side of inner truth. What especially pleased me was how instantly I *knew* each change, however minute. I was able to look in the mirror suddenly and within a second absolutely recognize what I saw. I was no longer the great mystery to myself that I had been. But I knew that I could go much further. I knew, after all, that however infinite these possibilities, their scope was relatively narrow. There were corners not explored by them. I suppose it was the crack that started me. Perhaps that was where I lost God, found the devil, and lost the courage to face myself. I don't know. The lower left side of the mirror had an eight inch crack. One day while rising from the floor I saw myself in that crack and began trembling. There was still another self! I had not seen it before. Ever. It was frightening, sinister. But my courage did not fail me then. From that moment I entered a new dimension of being. I split my image in a thousand ways. From top to bottom, sideways, diagonally, a fraction to the left side, my right eye only, from five feet away, my nose pressing the flawed surface. I was pleased, but often frightened, because although I saw new things I did not always understand. My mind was not equal to everything I saw, and my emotions did strange tricks. For example, on at least five occasions I had an almost overwhelming urge to slit my throat. Once I would have, but I could not find a razor. Do you know what it is like to want, very sincerely, to pluck out an eye? To want to see what is behind it? Do you see why I was frightened? But how could I turn back? Had I not begun a journey? I kept this up for six months. And then, it was late one winter evening, I got the idea to transfer what I saw in the cracked glass to the smooth. I lifted my head suddenly. Oh, God! I was looking at a monster! For five eternal, infernal minutes I looked. I could not break the cast, and I thought I should die. I was frightening myself to death. A cockroach crawled up the mirror, and as my eyes involuntarily followed it, my face relaxed. I did not go near the mirror for five days. It was odd that I should owe my life to a cockroach. I hated them. Some were so large they made noises. The first time I chased one under the door, I remember, as it squeezed through the tight space frantically, that it hissed! True, it was a kind of squishy hiss, no doubt the result of the particular situation. But it was an audible hiss, and unsettling. Other times they took shortcuts from the pipes overhead. Instead of crawling down a wall, they merely fell, landing on their backs with a sharp crack, and then scurried off. They were amazingly agile. Sometimes when I ran after one it seemed almost to float sideways as my foot came down. I have seen them zigzag, roll, reverse direction instantaneously, and jump. Surely their little legs did wondrous ugly things. I should have liked to grind them all into slime with boots. For a while I had a spray and would give them enough to immobilize but not kill them. They would roll over on their backs and twitch and move their legs, sometimes for hours. I conducted a very personal Inquisition. Days later I would not even notice their dried, crumbling bodies. But it became too time consuming to retaliate in this way, and they soon seemed to thrive on my poison. I went back to crushing them. When I returned to the mirror I did not attempt to transfer to the smooth mirror what I had seen in the cracked. That would have to wait until the very end, and even then I was not sure. Instead I attempted partial reconstructions of what I had seen. This was not, I discovered, without its dangers, but I learned to control my exposure and progressed very well indeed. I began with simple grimaces. I had dozens. Most of the variations came with the mouth and teeth. I alternated these with condescension, smirks, and minor irritations. These gradually led me into expressions of anger. I learned to flute my nose, bulge my eyes, and drain the blood from my face. In several months I developed a snarl that I could hold like a photograph for twelve minutes. My thoughts during such periods were much like nightmares. They were vivid, hard, compelling. I remember once I saw brilliantly colored electric saws cutting through thousands of writhing, screaming bodies. I felt smeared with blood: My ears could not bear the noise. And yet above it all there was laughter, loud ringing laughter. For a change I tried smiles, giggles, chuckles, chortles, sniggers, guffaws, titters, and hearty bellows. I was quite seductive in the beginning, especially with my coy and flirtatious smiles. But I always ended demonically, the development was always the same. This worried me a little. But then I reflected that true smiles are not natural with humans. Smiles were an affront to the bestial in us. I settled finally for those smiles which cut, those smiles which came out in the presence of pain and death. They seemed more consonant with truth. In my eighteenth month I moved on to madness. It was a natural progression. I contorted my mouth in a hundred ways. Sometimes I looked simple mad, other times dangerous mad. I had convulsions, I went catatonic. On a few occasions I had froth at the mouth like a rabid dog. In this phase I worked also with the voice and throat a good deal. I used words like "pussy," "candy," and "nice" with great effect. I discovered new veins, pulses, and twitches in my face and neck. One vein in particular, which ran along the left side of my face, was extremely impressive. It seemed always about to burst, and made my left eye so bloodshot there was no white left. I developed a little game at this time. I would stand with my back to the mirror, then suddenly turn and face my insane image. The shock value was very high.

Twice I fainted. And often I shrieked in spite of myself, responding as if I were quite another person. It was also at this point that I gave free rein to my lunatic laughs. I would explode into wild, chaotic warbles. This was the music of the earth when it erupted. I discovered new reaches to my vocal chords. My ears ached. My whole body went numb under the echoes of disintegrating noise. You think I must really have been mad? You don't know. You are too cozy in your nest. You think, what a ridiculous thing to do. What if someone heard you? Yet I know you have been tempted. Every now and then you look in the mirror and feel an anarchic impulse. You smile, but the smile is crooked, and you stop with just a flash of fear, thinking, how silly, how indecorous. But one day, give way, just once. Break the protective bonds you have woven. Laugh at yourself with all the abyss that is in you. You can do it if you want to. And then, see how hard it is to stop. See how easy it is to snap the threads of what you thought was your life. You will not thank me, for you will never be the same. You will always thereafter look in the mirror with caution. You will never feel safe! Do you understand what knowledge I discovered? Would you still laugh at me? Would you *dare* to? I finally had to rotate the mirror so that I faced its wooden back. I was not surprised that I could see myself in it. Nor was I surprised that gradually I could perceive my grotesque image being burned into the wood permanently. I hesitated at this point. Something kept me back, some ineffable internal mechanism. Almost simultaneously I realized that I had been looking only at my head for two years. The rest of my body had not existed before the mirror. Then I began stripping each day. I began, naturally, with the obvious. I had been looking at my genitals for seven weeks when Melinda first came. She fitted in perfectly with my plans. Of course I was brutal to her. She deserved far better. She had a difficult home life. I believe she was Polish. Her family was severely theological. Whenever she came home after having been with me, her father beat her. Sometimes after he beat her he made love to her and then beat her again. She tried to minimize their love-making by saying that he was not her real father, that she was an adopted child. I never believed her. Her father would never have known about her visits if she had not told him. Melinda was very honest. She claimed she did not mind the beatings. But I know differently. With my cruelty in addition, she suffered. Her mind seemed to weaken. When, upon her arrival, I pulled her over the chair and threw her on the floor, she invariably hit her head in the same place. It never healed properly. There were scabs upon scabs. Part of it was always suppurating. And it got larger and larger. No wonder reason began in time to fail her. Yet she was faithful, even when I had long since ceased to desire her. By then her whole head was infected. Her flesh still had charms. She was, after all, under thirty. But that was all near the end. In the beginning she was love itself. Her head hardly bled. I adored her. I never knew how she found me, whether she had been searching during the two years since I first saw her on the corner of McCoomb Street, indeed how she got past my barricaded door. She always kept part of herself a mystery. I did not mind because I found it enormously stimulating. I never knew when she would come. But her timing was always perfect. So distinctly did I sense her coming that she never once found me facing her when she entered. It was always the back, the fleshy arms, the tumble over, and love. After our initial exertion, we relaxed. She would lie with her throbbing head in my lap as I tweaked her nipples. That was when she talked. Her voice was thin and metallic and her ideas were infantile, but it was all music to me. She spoke of her ambition to be a singer. She regretted that her step-sisters were so young because a sister trio, she felt, was very sure of success. She realized that she had not had voice training, but she sang all the time and learned all the new song hits. Sometimes, while lying there, she sang me one. I was never impressed but complimented her on her manner. I told her she was very sophisticated and would probably make a name for herself on the international scene. That always made her turn her head and mischievously lick my belly button. It was her way of being continental. Her parents, she said, were opposed to a singing career because there was too much immorality in it. They had heard stories about women who sang. It was as bad as the theater. One story she herself believed, about a certain French singer who had been raped in her dressing room and had died of venereal diseases while giving birth to a monster baby. I conceded that a girl would have to know how to take care of herself. But she, I hastened to add, certainly did not have to worry on that score. This was good for another lick. She seemed to love her parents very much in spite of their opposition. Her mother had once been a beautiful woman. But work and children had made her fat. She had never loved her husband. She had married young, and after the wedding night her life was laid out for her like a corpse. She was bound to the man who had made her a woman. Melinda confessed that she liked her father more than her mother did. When I prodded her a little she admitted that she liked it when he loved her even though she knew it was sinful. She reconciled this and other matters with her morality by saying that all singers, the really good ones, had a past. They needed it to give style to their singing. She could always tell about a singer's suffering from the way she sang. Some of them had only voices and training, but no past. She could hardly wait until what her father did to her showed up in her songs. In a way, she would immortalize him. She hoped he would be alive when she became a success. One of her favorite dreams was to be singing in a fancy supper club with her father at a ringside table. As she sang, her past would show, and tears would roll slowly down her father's cheeks. After the show he would come to her dressing room and be unable to speak. He would drop a single white rose in her lap and rush out, choking down his anguish and his deep admiration for her. All the rest of the evening she would cry at how sad life was. And then that evening too would become a part of her past. She would sing as she never sang before. People would stop eating, overcome by the suffering in her song. But after, they would feel better for it. They would be gentler, kinder, more noble. They would feel love bubbling in their breasts. And so the years would begin to pass. She would move from success to success, ever higher in her chosen profession, reaching the hearts of millions. But finally, one day, a telegram would arrive. "Come quickly. He is dying." She would fly to his side, a mature woman, smelling of spring. She would bring him—a white rose, and hold his feeble hand. The pulse would weaken, he would try to speak and fail. She would know what it was he wanted to say, and she would gaze into his eyes, giving him strength. The mouth would open. "Forgive me. Forgive me. I...I..." She would finish for him. "Love you!" she would whisper passionately, "Love you!" And then, just before the end, so inaudibly that she would have to put her ear to his crusted lips (but still the magic!), he would say, "Marry...Have children... God bless...God bless..." And then nothing. The eternal rictus. He would be gone. At his funeral she would sing. Something new would be in her voice, something deep, something tragic. Even as his body was lowered into the grave, he would come to life again in her song, "The Old Man Has Checked Out." Among the mourners would be the head of the municipal opera. He would hear her sing and beg her to come to the opera. Reluctantly, she would go, and, untrained as she was, she would sing all the great tragic operas in all the great capitals of the world. In every note she sang, her past would show. And she would be great because her past was full of suffering. In her middle years, when her fame was for all time, she would yield to the pleas of the opera head and marry. They would have a child, a beautiful man child, and she would name the child after *him*. She could do no more. At last their sin would be expiated. I did not always see the logic of what she said, and the dream varied in minor details from telling to telling, but I always enjoyed it thoroughly. She usually had several orgasms while reciting, and that of course saved me work. I was not, strictly speaking, a youth anymore. My pleasure took more effort than formerly and depended a great deal on habit. Sooner or later, depending on Melinda's rate of recovery, we got up and went to the mirror. Our best hours were spent there, and though I am sure Melinda was bewildered, she got her enjoyment from them. What we did was to continue where I had left off when she had first come. However, instead of contemplating my genitals we contemplated hers. It was not always easy, but because the mirror was flexible we had reasonable scope. At first I had her just stand there and leered. She blushed and her nipples were very confused, going back and forth from erections to pink moons. I taught her to endure my most lascivious glances and droolings without blushing. But no sooner had she mastered that then I tried out twenty laughs and jeers on her. I laughed sneeringly and pointed. I ridiculed her wrinkly little part. I mocked the pimples on her nipples. She became hysterically humiliated. I had to slap her often. It took many months before she could look in the mirror with a sense of security again. Then I had her turn around and bend over, looking into the mirror through her legs. She objected. I put a cigarette in her and inked eyes on her buttocks. She cried and begged me to throw her to the floor. Instead I bent over in the same way, backed into her, and we kissed, after which I laughed like a madman. I had her lie on her shoulders, her legs wide apart, while I conducted minute anatomy lessons with a spoon. Sometimes during her humiliations she had an orgasm and became confused. She did not know whether to yield to her pleasure or resist it. Once I sandwiched a sausage between her buttocks and took a real bite. She shrieked, after which we made love. It took us nearly a year before we were ready for mutual pleasure before the mirror. She had by that time lost all shame and taught even me a few things. We used our fingers, our eyes, our tongues, our ears, our smell, our taste, our noses, our lips, our skin, our lungs, our hair, our knees and elbows, our teeth, our armpits, our mouths, our secretions, our muscles, our buttocks, our feet, and our toes to make love. We did it standing, crawling, squirming, kneeling, lying, squatting, jumping, rolling, upside down, hanging, running, and rotating. Once I blew into her organ and milk oozed out from her nipples. Another time she suckled my organ and became bloated like a blow fish until my orgasm. For nearly three years we made ecstatic, naked, complete love, all in front of the mirror. We were like gods. We could not lie. To be sure, there were times when I hurt her far too much. Once I nearly killed her. And the crack in the mirror and its possibilities haunted me. I dared not begin with that. But all this time Melinda's head got worse. In our fourth year together, she began to lose some of her hair, she put on a little weight, and her responses slowed down. She had begun voice lessons and talked more about her career. Her father invariably followed his beatings now with love. Melinda had so

varied her technique that in spite of herself she was driving him
insane. She said he was reading his *Bible* feverishly. My feelings
about Melinda eventually became ambivalent. In the beginning I
did not really think of her at all. I did dream of her. And when she
came, it was like a dream come true. I felt almost as if I had created
her. My wonderment lasted a long time. After all, when we had
met, so briefly and awkwardly on the corner of McCoomb Street,
she had manifested no instantaneous passion, no particular interest. She had been amused by my predicament. I remember that
for just a moment I had hated her intensely. What right had she to
smile at me? Why did she assume she could get away with it? Her
smile, after all, was a violation of my privacy, my person. It made
me an object of her amusement. I resented that. She should not
have noticed, or showed me that she noticed. I could not help at that
moment but be aware of her youth and beauty, her strength and
promise in contrast to my life-burdened self. Seeing the roundness
of her breasts and buttocks, the gold of her flowing hair, I felt a
mixture of passion and anger. I had the impulse to take the ice
cream wrapper and, laughing, shove it with my fist up her vagina.
But all this took place within a second. Our eyes barely crossed. My
mind quickly became immersed in other matters. Later I realized
that even in that short space of time she had crawled into my mind,
that fate had laid its tangles, and we were doomed to struggle out a
part of our life within them. My own response to Melinda during
the first two years I can reconstruct fairly well, even though she
existed only in my dreams. It was more difficult to find out what
she had thought. Perhaps I should never have pursued it because it
helped to shatter the bloom of our romance. Her first impression of
me, I discovered very late in our relationship, was that I was an
impresario. It was my long hair and strange manner (?) that made
her think so. She was convinced that I had to deal frequently with
temperamental singers, and that the ice cream wrapper had been
the last straw in a trying day. She thought that she had smiled
coquettishly, though in fact she had not. Obviously even then she
had had her ridiculous idea of a singing career. What happened
after is not so clear to me. I understand that it was important for

130

her to find me because I was necessary to her career. Incidentally, it argues for a commendable flexibility that when she discovered I was not an impresario she quickly put me to good use as part of her past. It just occurs to me now that I was therefore no different from the others before me. I just lasted longer. Why, I'm not sure. I originally thought Melinda came to me virginal in body, mind, and spirit. It was true only in the second, and she remained so to the end. Her spirit had become corrupt long before she met what she thought was an impresario, namely me. And her body became unspeakably corrupt in the two years she searched for me. The first several months after our fatal encounter, Melinda haunted the corner of McCoomb Street, hoping for another glimpse of me. She had somehow learned the truth that fate has few favorable turns and one must therefore make the most of each one. She could not know, however, that I had determined never to see McCoomb Street again. Quite naturally some of the men in the neighborhood thought she was there for reasons of prostitution. They were wrong. Melinda never charged. She was always delighted to go with a stranger because the more contacts she made the greater likelihood of finding her impresario. A great many demands were thrust upon her, but she was equal to them all. In a way, considering the variety of her opportunity and experience, I count it a compliment that she remained faithful to my image. But not a very large compliment. Occasionally, when I could convince her that I harbored no bitterness, she discoursed on her exploits. She had been most fond of a man called, unaccountably, Ding-Dong. He was a working man, and she had admired his thick, stumpy fingers. My own were quite slender. Ding-Dong had a mouse of a wife and he insisted that they all three get into bed together. His tastes were bizarre. When he lay atop Melinda, he had his wife astride his back, and they all bucked and yipped like cowboys at a rodeo. Melinda felt quite guilty about everything and spent a lot of time helping the mousey wife with the dishes and cleaning. She also wanted to make love to her by way of compensation, but the woman would have none of it. Only once, when she still smelled from the sweat of Ding-Dong, had she come close to succeeding.

But at the last moment the woman leaped out of bed and came at her with a nail file. Melinda never went back. The police, of course, became interested in her, but when they discovered she was not a professional they became friendly and invited her to several poker parties. At one, she was raped by every one of them (they were not in uniform) and at another she did monkey tricks on the table while the rookies ate pretzels from between her legs and laughed. This went on, in one way or another, for eighteen months. By that time, Melinda had slept with someone from every house but two on McCoomb Street. One house was inhabited by two very old spinsters, who steadfastly repulsed her overtures. They were rheumatic. The other was inhabited by Mrs. Maldive. She also resisted Melinda's charms. Her passions were, at the time, totally involved with me. However, under the pressure of my callous indifference, she began to pour out her troubles to Melinda. Melinda was ecstatic. She recognized me at once in Mrs. Maldive's tale of woe. She gave prayers of thanks for her success, knowing that through her she would eventually reach me. It was not, however, to be an easy path. Mrs. Maldive nourished in her fat heart an enormous capacity to absorb the buffets of life. Melinda became my substitution. Not that Mrs. Maldive relinquished her efforts to get at me. No. But in her waiting, she consoled herself with Melinda. On what passed between her and Mrs. Maldive, Melinda was silent. No threat could make her confess. It did not matter. My imagination supplied most of the details. I could see Melinda, naked, lying limp in the folds of Mrs. Maldive's naked lap, being plucked by greedy fingers. What unspeakable scenes they must have enacted on the bed! Whenever I thought of those wallowing scenes, I realized acutely the perverted immensity of Melinda's ambition. She *deserved* to succeed. But only gradually did a truth even more horrible dawn on me. It never occurred to me until our fourth year together to ask Melinda *how* she had persuaded Mrs. Maldive. Once Melinda had provoked her saurian lust, Mrs. Maldive would never let go. She would never, in repayment, offer her me. She would grant no request, no matter how tantalizingly couched. Melinda refused to clear the matter up. Obviously she had been successful. Then, suddenly one day, I *knew*! Melinda's visits to me were always preceded by visits to Mrs. Maldive! They had to be. Before she made love with me she made love with Mrs. Maldive. And she obviously made love so passionately to Mrs. Maldive that she left that sebaceous mass prostrate for hours afterwards, time enough for her to repeat the process with me. In this light, I almost saw Mrs. Maldive, her poor spent flesh quivering, as a *victim*. But it was still worse. After Melinda left me, she made love with her father! Oh, Melinda, Melinda! O fiendish ambition! I nursed this monster revelation for nearly a year. Honesty compels me to say that it did not lessen my pleasures. In fact, it increased them appreciably. The thought of the recuperating hippo, the idea that Melinda came to me dripping, as it were, from another exertion of love, the vision of her father's apoplexy, all these gave bouquet, added piquancy to our labors. And of course I was mindful always of her sacrifice, her selflessness. She endured Mrs. Maldive for *me*. She could not possibly have enjoyed her. I sometimes, I confess it, deliberately sniffed out the lingering mal-odors of my landlady, and was whipped by them into a frenzy of hate and passion. I cannot really say I lost by Melinda's promiscuity. Yet when one day she told me that her big break had come, that a burlesque house had promised to let her sing if she would do it nude while a comedian made obscene gestures behind her, I was perfectly cold and indifferent. I behaved as if I had suffered already too much by her behavior. I told her to go, that I had no need of sluts, that she was too old and used anyway. I surprised even myself. She cried, and we made love. She continued to come for several months, but the end had come. She stopped finally. The oddest thing about it all was that she was right. She had always been right. Melinda had had the clearest vision of all. When she began to sing, her past showed, and she rocketed to success. She quickly caught on in the movies, and I have no doubt she will make grand opera. She is already a fixture on television and considered quite a wit. Her head has never healed. But she has money, and the infection is carefully scraped away each day and hair pasted over it. The blood on my floor covers quite a large area now. Towards the end she bled rather freely. Sometimes

I lie down by it and remember the beauty that once was mine. Melinda, Melinda! My love for you was deep. My love for you was pure. Where have you gone? She was beauty and love, and I scorned her. And now she has left me to my horrible fate. It is, in a way, her fault. I do bear her this small bitterness. It was sometime after I had issued Melinda her quietus and we were in one of our cohesions of love. I had thrown her to the floor and done my usual. Then I rolled her onto me and gazed blissfuly at the ceiling, a little of her blood oozing onto my neck. But my bliss was short, for as I gazed, I saw the ceiling heave and pant until I thought it should break. I lost my erect status and scrambled out from Melinda, cursing her incompetence. She had been less than effective with Mrs. Maldive, and this was the result. *She had seen it all!* Now I was not only the great source of her frustration but also the robber of her consolation. I trembled at the thought of what Mrs. Maldive would do to me. Especially when Melinda no longer returned. Desperately I turned to her to beg her not to go. But she was gone already. She had quietly picked herself up, gathered her rags, and gone away. And I, I was alone with the pulsating ceiling and the sweating, sucking thing above it.—Ah, Melinda! Melinda!

Fragments

I DON'T SEE HOW I CAN MAKE YOU UNDERSTAND THE complete horror of what finally happened without telling you something about my past. My mother was a child bride and bore me, after prolonged labor, in her fifteenth year. She had had one miscarriage and one stillborn before me, and indeed, in my first few minutes of life they feared that I, too, was stillborn. But I was not. It was my earliest demonstration of cunning. Being weak and defenseless, I feigned death, and consequently was not harmed. It was a useful trick, to which I added many variations. For example, from an early age I was adept at hiding, which skill saved my life many times, I am sure. I could squeeze into unimaginable places and remain deathlike for hours. I rejoiced to hide under my parent's noses and listen to them call for me angrily. I was, naturally, the envy of my playmates when we played hide and seek. I could hide behind a blade of grass. Once I found a place so snug that only by curling could I get in. The others were quickly found and then all searched for me. Of course in vain. I waited until I thought I would burst, then tried to leap out laughing triumphantly "Here I am." But I could not. I quickly realized that I was *locked* in the abandoned refrigerator. Fortunately I did not panic. I took it as a challenge. I curled up even tighter. I sweated so much I seemed to be in a pool of liquid. I began to breathe very slowly and enjoy the dark and the heat. The walls became my friends, they protected me. I felt myself sinking into the dark infinite past. Trilobites crawled by me and the heavens opened up to reveal vast turbulent spaces. When the door opened, I was furious, though apparently too weak to vent my fury on anyone. I spent the next two days in bed being coddled and cuddled by my child-mother. She was a lovely thing. Big rubbery breasts, hard nipples, a faint smell of day old underwear, and a wet mouth. I loved her dearly. I was not toilet-trained until I was seven.

It made my first year of school difficult. The other children jeered at me. They would form a ring around me and dance, chanting, "Caca! Caca! Caca!" In class the whole room was permeated by my smell. The children giggled. They were used to it. But my spinster teacher was nearly prostrate from humiliation. She held a perfumed handkerchief to her nose, but that made teaching difficult. During music we all thought she would accidentally swallow it. Finally she forced herself to clean me up. She gave the children busy work and took me into the clothes closet. She was very put out the first few times and cried once when her finger got dirty. Then she became quite expert. We took longer and longer in the clothes closet, and later in the year, when I was finally getting the knack of holding my faeces in, she would come by my desk, but her lips in my ear, and whisper urgently, "Going to make nice caca today?" I had come to like her, for she was a good teacher. I tried to oblige, but the truth is that I was beginning to find it all a sticky business. When it became clear that I was finished with my infancy, she became frigid toward me, and ultimately cruel. At the end of the year I was the only pupil to whom she did not say goodbye. I cried bitterly. I tried to tell my mother but did not have the words. It did not matter. She held me close and consoled me. It was on this occasion that I really became aware that my father often glared hatefully at me when I was in my mother's arms. I am positive that at night he would come into my room and look at me. I always pretended to be asleep. I knew that if I were awake something terrible would happen. He was much older than my mother. Had she been a few years older she might well have refused him, although in all honesty I can't be certain. She was always a little slow mentally. Not that this showed or mattered. She had highly developed instincts and knew in her flesh ten times what other people knew in their heads. When my father had opened his fly and offered her the adult world, she was awed. It took only a few minutes for her to realize the benefits he could bestow. Her parents did not object. She had menstruated at eight, and by the time she was thirteen they were glad to be rid of her. They were displaced peasants and saw no particular virtues to further education for a girl. My father enjoyed swatting me on the head. The way I fell over made him laugh. My mother felt sorry for me, but she was too afraid of him. She began to hug me only in private, but it was better because she hugged me more passionately. I came to hate him very much, especially because I knew that my mother still liked him in certain ways, even when he hit me. I trace the genesis of my plan to that period. I got my revenge on him. When I was nearly sixteen years old, my mother had a baby girl. My father was overjoyed. She was a blond fairy-child, and he played with her constantly. She was his princess, his doll, his little frog. I had been none of those things. He still punched me every opportunity he got. For some months I tried weight-lifting, hoping to put on enough weight and muscle to beat him to a bloody mass. But it was hard work. There was hardly any change. And he was so big. Then I thought I would castrate him in his sleep with a rusty razor. I soon abandoned the idea because I knew he rarely slept with my mother any more. He had in fact withdrawn considerably into himself as his potency waned. He moved into a room upstairs because he could not face the ripeness my mother still had. Only when drunk did he attempt any conquest. When the baby came he was agog with hope, and I bided my time with secret joy. I wanted to speak only when my words would crush him. I did not have to wait long. When the girl was six months old, I was deceived one day by the tone in his voice. He had the child in his lap and asked me to hold her for a minute. I had never been allowed to touch the child in his presence, and I hesitated. He smiled, and I felt on the verge of tears as I went forward. The past years of cruelty dissolved, and hope bloomed monstrous and quick in my heart. And then, just before I touched the child, his fist shot out, knocking me across the room and onto the floor. "You dirty cockroach," he said softly, "don't you ever touch her." I never forgot his words, never. I laughed hysterically. I was disconcerted at the shrieking quality of my laugh. It was not the laugh I had planned. I had difficulty in stopping, but at last I was silent, the words ready inside my mouth. We looked at each other with primeval hatred. I opened my mouth venomously, viciously, to speak. And then fear ripped my tongue and forced the shreds down my throat. I choked. More clearly than

I had ever known anything before, I knew that he knew the words, that he was waiting to hear them, that he would kill me as soon as I said them. I did not want to die. I got up and rushed out the door under his laughter. Turning, with tears in my eyes, I whispered fiercely, "She's not your child! She's not your child!" But it was too late. The moment had passed. I spent the night with my mother. She was very kind. Two months later I succeeded. I took the child one night and put it in the trunk of a car going east. I wrapped the baby warmly and gave her a bottle of milk with a little wine to make her sleep. Then I returned, took the longest knife we had, and stuck it in his door. I gathered my favorite objects and a few clothes and left. It was the beginning of a new phase of life for me. I became a hobo for nine years. During that time I gained most of my education, superficial as it was. I learned from traveling, from being on the move. I learned from the hoboes I met. I learned from the odd scraps of reading that came my way. The traveling was dirty but good. I saw America the best way—free. I got close to the wheels of progress, but never turned them. My companions were the best in the world. Our ties were non-existent. We had no loyalty, no expectation. They had all crawled out from the bottom of life and spewed out the pimples, boils, infections, ulcers, and vomit that had been their lot. Of course they escaped nothing. Their freedom was an illusion. Inside they rotted. The very perimeter of life which they skirted so skillfully was testimony to their dull agonies. I changed my name frequently, fearing that someone would know me if I used my real name. Some of the names I used were Abner Thurls, Gaylord Harrington, Tyrone Ginsberg, Pauli Svaboda, Mike Pilzner, and briefly, Murial. There was another reason for my many names. I sought release from myself. I tried to imagine a personality to fit each name. I think my Svaboda incarnation was the most successful. I was a happy Hunky. I told jokes. I slapped backs. Nothing bothered me, neither rain, nor hunger, nor police. These last were particularly hard on us. A hobo is the man most without identity. He has no social security, no bank book, no letters, no documents of any kind. He has no address, no family or relatives that exist for him. He is going nowhere, he has come from nowhere. He follows no clock, daily or seasonal. His most discernible characteristic is a rigid adherence to nothingness. Nothing must matter. If anything mattered, it was a step back. Of course the fact that things must not, rather than do not, matter gives him away. In some remote part of him, things do matter. That is why he is not truly outside society but on the perimeter, desperately on the perimeter. He nourishes a hope, secret even to himself except at stray moments, that somewhere somehow there will be a chink just his size and he will slip smoothly in again and live. But this vestige was too remote for people inside the perimeter to perceive. They saw us as threats, as foreign agents of an invisible but powerful empire. They sicked their minions in blue on us. And they in turn beat us, booted us, locked us up, and robbed us. In the end they always let us go, hustling us out of town at sunset because whatever they did to us did not visibly decrease our potency for them. Rather it increased. Our seeming indifference to their abuse frightened them. Our black empty world terrified them. The image of men sitting, traveling, sleeping, saying little, caring for nothing, silhouettes at dusk in a wasteland—it was too much to bear for long. It challenged the logic of work and family and community. We knew our power and always had the patience to wait. One place was as good as another. Later we would joke without sincerity. It did not matter. And that was what was wrong with Pauli Svaboda. I joked as if I'd gotten a real thrill out of besting the police. I felt proud when I did not shiver in the cold. I expected praise when I stole a chicken. I was a Judas, I betrayed them. I behaved openly as if things did matter. I was dimly aware that I had stirred my companions to a vague irritability and contempt, but it was not until one morning when I woke up alone that I realized how much of a failure Svaboda was. I had just turned nineteen. I was too young to have used up a life already. I always managed to send post cards and letters when I changed my name, both to my mother and father. Naturally the ones to my mother were loving and tender. Those to my father were poisonous. I murdered him a thousand times in my dreams. In the beginning I was desperate for release from my memories and read everything I could. I read a great many true love and true confession magazines, but mostly I read comic books. Flash Gordon, Superman, Prince Valiant, Captain Marvel, The Phantom—these names stirred me. I liked Prince Valiant best of all because I lusted after his wife. When she had a child I was annoyed. I thought back desperately to when it could have happened. But I could not remember any night when they were alone together in bed. I was disgusted with the deception of having her conceive between issues. The relations of my other heroes with women was cool, and distant, even formal. The girls were pretty and healthy, and you knew they would keep. There was no danger of sexual violation. Your dreams were safe. But Prince Valiant's blond wife was slender and always in need of protection. She was made for a warrior to sleep with after he had slain swarthy enemies. I hated him for trespassing on her frailty, not because he had not the right, not because she was not pre-eminently desirable, but because she should have waited for me. I reveled in the long periods that he was away from her; it was my only consolation. We passed many lurid nights that her creator never imagined. Of course all this was not healthy. I lived, in the beginning, far too much in fantasy. For over two years I was the strong and silent type. Whenever I came or left I did so urgently, always looking over my shoulder for enemies or retainers. I took up spitting. I said little but tried to have eyes blazing with knowledge. I did not have the right physique, so I hunched my shoulders. I smoked only butts, even when I had whole cigarettes, and developed a heavy tread. On a wooden platform I could sound like an elephant. I found leaning on a tree a good posture, and learned to look alternately scornful and pitying. One day a very small man came up behind me, gave me a pointed kick in my rectum, said "Move yer ass, buddy," and lay down to sleep. When I realized I should have struck him it was too late. My image, the product of twenty-four months of careful attention, had been shattered. It was time for another incarnation. I became a loner, but I began to masturbate so much I was afraid I'd go crazy. It was Kronka who finally broke the spell for me. Kronka was unusual in the hobo world. Most of the men are sexually neuter. Their senses are dulled They are not interested in anything except occasional masturbation. However, a fair number of them are interested in sex with each other, and young men are attractive to this type. It is not a very feminine sexuality, there is no flittiness, no swaying of the hips, no eyes, just a question of holes and parts to fit them. There is no romance to it at all. Sometimes it is bestial, but never passionate. I confess that for a brief period I thought homosexuality was the solution for me. I went so far as to call myself Murial, a name I had always admired and endowed with all the sweetness of womanhood. I effected a girlish manner and rolled my pants to my knees. Once I even shaved my legs. I came upon a small group one day at sunset on the weedy outskirts of Kansas City and wiggled into the center of them, talking nervously about the heat and how difficult it was to move my bowels anymore without an audience, such was reputation. They were silent and allowed me to feed from the common pot. They left me alone after the meal, and though I chattered constantly, no one answered me. There were, however, many covert looks. It had been dark several hours when I gave up and walked toward the woods to urinate. One of the men tripped me, and then several of them jumped on me, beating me mercilessly as they cursed, "Fucken homo! Fucken homo!" I crawled away to the wood and wept silently as the blood dried. I heard a noise next to me, and before I could beg the man not to beat me again he was on top of me muttering in a crazy guttural voice, "Come on, honey. Be a sweetie now." I had no strength to resist. After him came seven others. They had me both ways. I had every pain. The last one was a surprise. He wanted me to have him. When I laughed feebly he beat me unconscious. He must have been brutal then, because in the morning I was unable to move. I was covered with blood and for weeks I ached when I moved my bowels. That was my punishment for rousing the specter of passion in them. They were all gone, of course. I just lay there, waiting to die. It was Kronka who found me. He was a giant. I looked up at the sky and there he was. I knew he would kill me. Then he laughed. "Looka the birdie," he said. He washed and fed me for six days until I was well. In all that time he said nothing but "Looka the birdie." He obviously was not interested in me sexually. I soon came to know that Kronka was one of the few hoboes with an urgent lust for females. I first realized how urgent it was one day when he had been staring at a picture in a magazine for hours. I could see he had been nursing an erection. Finally he came over to me and threw the magazine down. I trembled. He knelt down and jabbed the picture, which was of a nude woman with one leg raised so that the knee covered her pubic area. His eyes were blazing. "See!" he said. "Dere's de cunt! Dat dere's de cunt!" He stood up, took out his enormous organ and thrust it through the picture, letting out a howl. He left the pierced pin-up on him and went crashing through the woods. I knew he would copulate with the first female he met, be it farmer's wife, a moose, a pheasant, or a rabbit. He was very much a wild man. Even when he was not desperate, he had a primitive approach to the female. He would often come up to a farm house and knock. If a woman answered, from nine to ninety, Kronka would open his fly and hold his penis in his hand with a sly smile. He was remarkably successful in this ploy. First of all, he seemed able to smell the woman in heat. If he made a mistake, the woman just slammed the door, even if her husband were at home. Kronka would only have crippled or killed him. There were all kinds of women. Some screamed. Some politely said no, thank you. Some cried. A few laughed. Once one swung at it with an axe. Kronka put it away and went off laughing. Sometimes the woman took it out of his hand as if it were a salami he was selling and pulled him in. Other women carried on a conversation for their husbands' benefit while pointing to the barn or shed or woods. Once, when a young girl answered and was very taken with Kronka, her mother came, slapped her, and drove Kronka into the woods with a broom. There she lay with him under a tulip tree while the daughter and I played in the kitchen. Kronka had no taste whatsoever in females. He could look at a cow, point, and say "Dere's de cunt" with as much libido as if it were a beautiful woman. He loved all females in creation. I have seen him look with as much interest at a farmer's livestock magazine as at a girlie magazine. He generally went after women because they were easier to handle and easier to get at than livestock. He haunted county fairs whenever he could. He walked through the sheds and pens with a look that would have marked him as a raving sex maniac had they been women instead of sheep, pigs, and cows tied there. At night he would slip away alone, coming back in early morning to sleep off his sodomite orgies. I am certain he left many a puzzled farmer in his wake. He had managed, in his pursuits, to pick up a lot of comparative anatomy. Although I felt it was often wrong, I was not experienced enough to challenge him. For example, when he picked up a grasshopper and poked it with his finger, saying, "Dere's de cunt," how could I contradict him? Especially since he usually crushed it in the process. I often wondered what he would do were he near the ocean. I have imagined him with lobsters, squid, whales, and walruses. Had he wings, no bird would have been safe from him. Naturally, I never told him about Prince Valiant's wife. I liked Kronka and was very deeply sorry when he got himself killed. We had been doing a particularly desolate and scrubby stretch in Arkansas. It was turning cold, and Kronka had been unable to find anything at all for release. It was a poor state. I became apprehensive, but needn't have. Kronka would never have touched me. He began moaning one night and looking at the trees around us. He had his usual monstrous erection sticking out of his pants. I sensed his frustration. He could not figure out the anatomy of the trees, he did not know where the "cunt" was. His eyes were streaked with red. Suddenly he went roaring down the track. I pitied whatever should be in his path, man or beast. I went to sleep listening to him howling in the distance. When I awoke he had not returned. I waited until noon, then set off in search. I was worried. Towards sunset I found him. He was caked with blood all over. His face was smashed in. Nothing but a train could have done that to Kronka. I saw everything. I saw the darkness. I heard the whistle. Then the light piercing the black, and Kronka, running wildly over the ties with his lance, bellowing, "Dere's de cunt! Dere's de cunt!" until the blinding consummation that must have thrilled him even as it destroyed him. I rolled him over to search his pockets and saw that his penis had been ripped away. He had three cents, a thimble, and a horse racing magazine. I rolled him into the gully by the tracks and walked away. I wondered why I did not feel sad, why I had not cried or said a prayer or simply sat by the body in shock. It was not until two days later that I realized I could remember very little of my life before I met Kronka. I tried often, but I always failed. My past was a blank except for a few erotic visions and a terrifying father who stalked me endlessly. Why? Why? I wandered about the country for another fifteen months, hoping to meet with faces and circumstances that would enlighten me. I did not. Nothing changed. During all that time, Kronka's death weighed heavily on me. I could not recapture the peace and security I had felt with him. I tried to imitate him but could not. The farmers' wives only laughed at what I showed them. I did not have Kronka's sense of smell, I did not have his gigantic zest. I was nothing. I did not even have a name. When Kronka had found me I was Murial. In all the time I was with him he called me Birdie, which I found satisfactory. I decided to appropriate Kronka's name though I knew it was a meaningless sacrilege. One early spring evening I stopped at a car dump in northern Mississippi. It was godforsaken but for the wrecks of cars. The dump extended for miles on one side of the tracks. The other side was mainly swamp. It was filled with cranes, herons, egrets, snakes, small mammals, and insects. Each night a freight train brought hundreds more into a siding. From there they were lifted up and swung out into the dump. Some were driven or towed in along a rutted dirt road that wound for five miles before it reached pavement. Its only other use was by Saturday night lovers. I chose a remote corner to settle down in. There was work going on, of course, but far off. I heard the cars being crushed and reloaded on freight cars, saw them leave like coffins, but I was rarely disturbed. Only twice in five years did I have to move. I originally settled in a 1939 Dodge, but when I realized that I could have my pick I chose those cars that stimulated my imagination. I lived in a Pontiac and a DeSoto. I lived in America's past glory. By siphoning other wrecks I was able to have a steady supply of gas, which I used to run the motor of the wreck I lived in. This gave me heat when I needed it, hot water, and a stove of sorts. I was not interested in a radio; I had the stars. There were many rats, but when they realized that I meant to live with them and that I meant business they left me alone. There was enough for all. It was an idyllic life. The nights were warm and peaceful much of the year, the swamp sounds were lulling. The workers went home, the crane was locked in its incline, and as night fell it looked like a sad petrified dinosaur. I was well protected from the rain. The sound of it on thousands of rusting hulks was a delicious symphony. I was comfortable and reasonably happy. I caught fish, snared rabbits, picked berries and greens, and occasionally found cans and boxes of food and candy bars in the wrecks. Heinz, Campbell, Nabisco— such names became the identifications of prized fossils. Searching the wrecks occupied a good deal of my time. I not only searched the trunks and glove compartments, but also under the seats and inside the seat covers. I amassed a small fortune in this way, mostly in coin and small bills. But there were a few surprises, like the ten one hundred dollar bills I found in an empty crumpled cigarette package on the floor of a 1935 Ford. I also accumulated a library. Of magazines, of course, there were many. But the number of books was stupifying. No one ever removed books from a wreck. They were interred with the blood and the upholstery. Merely citing at random, I had twenty volumes of *US Fisheries and Hatcheries*, Almanacs for the last fifteen years, the complete novels of Yancy Stringer, of which *Powder Your Nose* was by far the best, the poetry of Catullus in Latin (which I did not know), sixty-nine *Bibles*, *A Memoir of Jacques Louis David* (in French, which I did not understand), *Plots of the Great Operas*, *Eating for Old Age* by Cora Yeobright, and *The Principles of Carpentry* by Olaf Olaf. There were also thousands of comic books. I read slowly and deliberately, most often during the hot part of the day, and even became a scholar of sorts. It was a great solace to me. I enjoyed history and biography most. If I could not fill in my own past, I could at least sponge on the past of others. The only thing I missed was someone to talk to. I itched to try out my new found knowledge. It was quite by accident that I discovered I was not alone in the automobile graveyard. I had wandered one day further than usual during my constitutional. I had long ago given up any hope of exploring the entire area. But I occasionally enjoyed a foray into unknown territory. While negotiating a particularly bad wreck, a 1938 Chrysler, I caught my foot and bent down to free it. I found myself looking into two eyes and nearly broke my leg trying to leap out. I could not. Still fearful, I bent down again. The eyes had not moved. "Who are you?" I asked. "Jeb," he answered. "Do you live here?" "Yep." He was a small and wiry man. His eyes were large and alert. He seemed faintly amused. "How long have you been here?" I asked. He paused, then cackled loudly. "Ask Old Pete," he said, *"ask Old Pete."* He darted out the other side of his car and disappeared. I surprised him there a few more times, but got little out of him. He would not tell me where he lived. He had been there fifteen years, and he was a new-comer. Others had been there much longer; Old Pete, who was some kind of Patriarch, the longest. There were secrets, he implied, I would learn if I stayed long enough. I met several more like Jeb, all accidentally, all equally elusive. They were not interested in talking. It was not that they were afraid of me or even anti-social. They simply did not need me. They were quite happy alone. They were not much of an outlet for my desire to communicate, but they started me thinking about new things. These men were different from hoboes. For one thing, they were stationary. For all the indifference of hoboes, one always felt they were running. These men were not. They had resolved something. You felt no sense of unrest about them, no vague desperation or loss. They had left the perimeter. They had learned something. For that reason they were terrifying. They had gotten outside life and society by going into the midst of it, where death smelled eternally fresh. The miles of junk were as central as a hospital or a cemetery. The new cars each week were like news bulletins. By examining them you could tell about the hearts of those outside. You could tell lesser things too, like on which seats love had been made, whether children had played in the car, whether a woman had driven the car, how fat she was, the relative prosperity, the religious and cultural attainments of the owners, how badly injured the driver had been in the crash, and so on. The cars were like a pulse to the country. But so far as I could tell, Jeb and the others were not interested in these facts; they constituted their ancient history. They had moved far beyond any cynicism or despair. They truly did not care. I do not think there were any women. At least I never saw one. This culture was self-immolating, and happily so. What they did day and night I never found out. Probably what I did. But I can't be sure. My thoughts, as I said, were new. First of all, the prospect of never leaving did not alarm me. It was even pleasant. That I should, for all practical purposes, disappear from the face of the earth was perfectly acceptable to me. In a sense, it seemed that by living where I did I had already reached the end most people were striving for and could therefore have the leisure to relax and contemplate. Here I could live with a truth equal to the anguish of life. I did not bother about the far distant problem of what I should do when the junk city became overpopulated, as it inevitably would. I was lucky to be one of the early ones. My meditations were pessimistic, but, oddly, brought me great peace of mind. When a child, and even when a hobo, I had cuddled the notion that even though things were bad there was an ideal good toward which all was striving and which would ultimately be achieved. Perhaps this was what made me a bad hobo. Perhaps all hoboes were looking for the right junk yard, and I had by some grace been enabled to bypass all their wandering years. I don't know. I don't really think so. I had seen all evil in the light of this good and took comfort in the belief that all would eventually be corrected. I vaguely connected God with this good and saw Him as working out his perfect plan in His own devious but certain way. Here among the smashed cars and dried blood I began to doubt. Not so much God as myself. I thought about the blood and the broken heads. I thought about candy bars and radios. I thought about the hula girls who danced in the rear windows and the virgins and St. Christophers who gazed serenely out the front windows. Above all I thought of the weekly additions that became, with day and night and the seasons, part of the new clock by which I regulated myself. I began to think that I had been a fool. There was, for example, no redemption for my father. His cruelty was not mitigated by the kindness it might have been. He was merely cruel, and I merely suffered; both were written on time. Had I known more I might not have suffered so much, for it was, after all, the vision of something better that made it all so painful. Instead of facing and accepting that dark shadow over my bed, I had yearned after the good like a love sick school boy. And was it not true everywhere? The smashed cars were real. One could not have a car without damaging it in this world. Death and destruction, decay and dissolution were built into it, into us. That truth was all around me. Even if one kept it locked in a garage, it would rust and rot. One had always to see the junkyard in the end, and order his life accordingly. It was really so simple I wondered why people did not see it. It made life a great deal less and a great deal more at the same time, harder but easier. The cars led me into people's hearts, and what I saw in the junkyard I saw in their hearts also. This was a different God I envisaged, if God he was. But I was, I soon discovered, nowhere near the thoughts of Old Pete. After four years among the wrecks I began to think Old Pete was a myth. He was not. There was one area of the yard I never thought of going near because the cars there were so old they had been abandoned even by the junkyard. Where I could identify at all I saw ghosts of Stutz, Cord, Pierce-Arrow, the early Fords, Doble. Some had even returned to dust. I saw nothing to be gained there, no money, no food. Yet one day I found myself wandering there, almost by irresistible impulse. It was a larger area than I imagined, and I got quite lost in its maze. I could not see over the cars but did not worry. All that was needed was to climb up and look. I was about to do just that when I saw something shining in a hole at my foot. I bent down and saw that an entire car was buried so that its roof was at ground level. The hole was big enough to squeeze through, and I did, scratching myself slightly. On the floor of the car I found a silver coin, which of course was extraordinary, considering the rust and decay all around me. I looked around for more and saw that next to this car were others, in all directions. It was an entirely new layer of cars. When I had thought myself walking securely on earth I had really been walking on the thinly disguised roofs of old wrecks. How precariously I had tread. I became intrigued with the possibilities and went into one car, then another. Irregular beams of light shone through and I thought myself perfectly safe. But when I started back I became hopelessly lost. I scurried frantically from car to car like a huge rat and finally lay down exhausted. I was cold and terrified by strange scratching sounds. I knew that dangerous snakes must be lurking near. The light was fading. I had been underground hours. Suddenly laughter burst out somewhere beneath me. I froze. "Come down," the voice said. I looked everywhere but saw no hole, no passage. "Lift the seat. Lift the seat." I did. there was only space beneath it. Then a round white face. It disappeared. "Climb down. Hurry." It was a thin, high-pitched voice, as if from withered vocal chords. I saw the ladder and descended. Below were more wrecks, but the passageways were distinct. The man before me was short, fat, and white. His whiteness was the color of certain fat worms under bark or logs. He wore a long black coat, very shabby and very shiny. I did not ask who he was. "I wondered when you'd drop in," he said. Then he laughed softly and toothlessly. "Come. Come on," he said, making quick inviting gestures. I followed him down several twists and turns, which led finally into a pitch black cave. He turned a key, a motor hummed, and ceiling lights overhead went on. They were the headlights of cars which he had cleverly arranged to light up every inch. They looked like monster eyes and I felt rudely made naked and succulent in their glare. Old Pete laughed and switched on the dims. His home was well furnished. He had arranged car seats into a sumptuous bed. His easy chairs were bucket seats. His bureau was a series of glove compartments welded together. His tables were steering wheels covered with glossy metal sheets. All around me were dismemberments from Bugatti, Dusenberg, Rolls Royce. "Sit down. Sit down, my boy," he said, pointing to a maroon bucket seat. We sat facing each other. He said nothing. He kept on chuckling to himself and rubbing his hands. A few times he poked between his legs vigorously. An occasional rat skirted by us. I was cold. I could not help feeling the weight of the entire junk yard above me. I expected it to collapse at every moment. His greedy look made me nervous. Just as I began to speak, he screeched joyfully, "From the beginning. Yes, from the beginning." He said nothing more for an hour. All I could make of the remark was that perhaps he had been entombed in the yard with one of the early wrecks. Finally he went and fetched a wheel. I could not believe it was a car wheel. It looked like a wagon or carriage wheel. Leaning forward, his eyes glistening, he said, "More below. More below." I thought for a minute he was going to take me, but he did not. I was not anxious to go into his cellars. I believe that they must be endless, and beneath even the Mors, Serpollet, and Gorbron-Brillie I envisioned curricles and brouettes lying over encrusted *quadrigae*. Although he was not large, he gave the impression of much fat or flab. It was the kind of fat which, if you squeezed it, would not resume its shape quickly. Perhaps, in his case, for hours. I had a momentary urge to mold his face into ridiculous forms. It was several more hours before I realized that Old Pete was not really chuckling. He was gloating. I did not understand, but it frightened me. He was like a fat, featherless hen sitting on an egg filled with worms and spiders. At last he stood up. "Come again," he squeaked. "Come again. I'll show you more." I nodded, got up, and looked confused. I had no idea where to go. He shrieked with laughter and led the way. When he stopped and pointed up I began to climb. From below, he said, "I'm rich! I'm rich!" I climbed faster. And when I was nearly out, "I'm a king! I'm a king!" His laughter died away. I ran over the tops of the cars without regard to my safety until I reached familiar territory. Then I stretched out on the roof of a car, took deep breaths while looking gratefully at the moon, and went to sleep. I had no intention of returning, but I did. Out of curiosity, I suppose. Jeb had mentioned secrets. I never learned them. For a short time I suspected that one of them was that Old Pete was a Jew or a Negro. I got no confirmation of this. The two times I saw Old Pete again, he was almost as silent as the first time. He gloated and rubbed his hands. He never stopped looking at me. On one visit, all he said, at long intervals, was, "Do you feel it? Do you feel it?" I knew he did not mean the lice, but did not ask him to elaborate. I guess I knew he would not. I finally did feel something, and it made me uncomfortable. It was crawling all around me, inside me, everywhere. It was in the air. I could not escape it. There is no way to describe it. I suppose it had something to do with the way he took the end product, the disaster product, of one world and molded it into a new one. He sucked up still bloody bones with bits of ragged flesh on them and smacked his lips. He saw hope and vitality where I saw revelation and warning. I was content to let my knowledge condition me to more realistic behavior in the world I knew, should I ever return to it. Old Pete took the ingredients of my knowledge and rejoiced in them. It was not enough for him to know about the black world; he wanted to live in it, to find his being in it. He had succeeded. The sun would have killed him, roasted him instantly, leaving only his shining black coat. Still, I knew that there was more to Old Pete than I could decipher. The last time I saw him he gave me a book. It was *Walden* by Thoreau. I had read it once, but never thought of it. He put it in my lap and patted it reverently. "My book," he said, "my book." Again we looked at each other a long time, he rubbing his hands and chuckling softly. Once he punctuated the silence with the statement, "Simplify." This moved him to peals of laughter. Another time he said, mysteriously, "Rock bottom. Rock bottom." Then he took me by the hand and pulled me down a long tunnel. It led to a dank and shadowy clearing. He switched on a flashlight, and I saw rats looking back at us more or less fearlessly. He seemed impatient at my fear, and I soon realized it was not the rats he wanted me to see. It was the mushrooms, thousands of them, some as large as tables, some as provoking and exotic as coral formations beneath the sea. Indeed some of them seemed to undulate, as if by the force of invisible waves. When he was convinced that I had seen, he pinched me and squealed. "Mine," he said, "all mine." He was very proud. On the way back he showed me a wall covered with copies of *Walden*. He began mumbling "Rock bottom" to himself over and over again. He did not see me any more, and I left. I reread the book he had given me but could not make sense of it. I could not abandon myself to the goodness and rightness of my nature. I could not feel the ultimate unity of all things. I could not feel myself comfortably in the lap of an immense beneficent deity who desired only my honest responses to life. To be sure, I shared Thoreau's aversions, but I did not feel free to ignore them as he did. Yet the book remained in my consciousness. I thought of it at odd moments. And ultimately I think Thoreau would have approved of me as he could never have approved of Old Pete. Or was it Old Pete who would not have approved of Thoreau? I don't know. They were both strange creatures, but they did not go together. Each one made it impossible for me to commit myself to the other. Yet Old Pete had somehow married himself to the man in the hut, the measurer of ice, the friend of chickadees. Did they share the same God? Sometimes I think Old Pete sucked on a huge joke. The idea made me shiver. Yes, he was sucking Thoreau as if he were a big lollypop. But why? Why did he bother? I think part of my difficulty was that I knew so little about Old Pete. What did he do when I was not with him? Of course he must have tended his mushrooms. But what else? Did he gloat and rub his hands all day or night? What were his activities, his involvements? Perhaps there was a wife and children down one of his tunnels. At the deepest levels, were there routes to other junkyards? Perhaps he prayed. Perhaps he played bridge, or poker, or some other social game. I really did not know. Without that knowledge, what could I say about him? Sometimes I did feel that I *knew* Old Pete. But I did not want to believe it because I was not sure I liked what I knew. I finally gave him up, as much as I could. I was still relatively young. Five years is not much time in which to learn anything that counts. I had not faced him fully. But then I had not faced myself fully either. I could not do the one without the other. I let it all alone. I began to think about the few scraps of my past that I remembered. But I could not extend them. They made no whole. I felt only guilt and a vague sense of pursuit. One day a train went by. I saw the beautiful face of a blond girl. She smiled at me. Before I could smile back, she was gone. Three weeks later I walked down the tracks after the train and never returned. I was determined to find that blond girl. I had something to do. I was convinced that she would help unlock my destiny.

Selected Correspondence

Washington, D.C.
July ----

Dear Father,

No doubt by now you have discovered I am gone. And where can your darling daughter be? I am working for the F.B.I. and have given them a complete file on you. Haw, haw. You are an impotent insect as well as a red.

Your loving son,
X

PS: Did you see the knife in your door?

Washington, D.C.
July ----

Dear Mom,

I dream of you every night and cry. Believe me, I had nothing to do with the baby's disappearance. I love you, I love you, I love you. Don't let him touch you. A million kisses. You are living with a swine.

Your son,
X

*

Rangoon
September ----

Dear Daddy,

I have decided you are a shithead. I haven't got the time to bother about you because I am on an assignment. Do you remember the time you deliberately stepped on my hand when I tried to pick up a penny you had dropped? Well, that hand is so strong now I can strangle a person with it. The fellers call it the King Kong hand! And where is your darling daughter now? *Your* darling daughter? Haw, haw. I am laughing myself sick. Don't wake up at night. You might see me.

Your obedient servant,
Abner Thurls

Ethiopia
September ----

Dear Mommy,

I am leaving the F.B.I. for the English Foreign Service. They need men who understand Arabs and are willing to undergo suicidal missions. If I live, I shall write. If I die, remember I love you. That is what preserves me.

Oodles of,
X

Tanganyika
September ----

Mums,

There is a stillness here at night that stirs my Polish blood. The wild howls and the constant struggles of life and death remind me of our gallant ancestors, so brutally oppressed, yet so courageously defiant. I cannot help but feel nobility in our line and I have decided to dedicate my life to restoration. I just killed a poisonous snake called a *fer de lance*. The area is *infested* with them, but believe me, they are the least of my troubles. Long live Poland!

(Mike)

Sioux City
Xmas ----

To my Father at Christmastide:
A bag of beans (to help him fart). A watermelon rind. Zebra stripes. One mouse trap. Toothpicks. Gunga Din. Salt water taffy. A green nightmare. Halitosis.

Chico

Cincinnati, Ohio
May ----

Dear Mom,
It is spring here and I have grown a lot in the last two years. I have not written because I have not stayed in any one place for more than a day. I am traveling with a grand bunch of fellows, very hale and hearty. We are on the high road to adventure day and night. We have a lot of fun and a lot of laughs. I have toughened up but remember you fondly. How is the old man? (??)

Your son,
(now) Abner Thurls

*

155

Sledge, North Dakota
June ----

O Daddy mine, don't ever sleep,
Your offspring's in the night,
And he will strike the scales of justice,
For right is right.

Abner Thurls (his mark)

The Alamo
June ----

Dear Father,

Where was God when the Alamo fell? How I weep for those men!

A.T.

Reno, Nevada
July ----

Dear Father,

I have been thinking and have decided that you are not to blame. Not that you are not a despicable human being. But I realize that you were *made* that way and no one could have changed you except God. I have found religion out here on the desert. *He* is with me everywhere. I can touch *Him* if I wish and speak to *Him*. *He* tells me to forgive you and I do. You must make your reckoning with Satan, and his realm is fire and everlasting pain. I know you hold against me what I did to mother, but that was only natural. She is closer in age to me than to you, and you cannot blame hot blood. God has forgiven me, as I forgive you, your trespasses. I shall pray for you in Hell. The girl is better off where she is, and one day I shall claim her as my own. Until then, I urge you to patience, goodness, and love of God, for *He* is Almighty.

Abner (also called Isaac)

San Diego, California
October ----

Mums,

Don't be surprised if you see me some night. It will be a secret visit but I am burning to disclose my plans to you. I know you will approve. I am a new person. I am a *natural* aristocrat of the earth!

Your loving and dutiful son,
(now) Gaylord Harrington

Ohio
November ----

Dearest Mother,

I am on the banks of our great Mississippi and am thinking of DeSoto. Westward lies the virgin land and all hope. Tomorrow I am setting forth on a glorious destiny. America is my future! I have shed my past. We have a great role to play, and I must be a part of it. You will hear of me.

Your true son,
Daniel B.

Pittsburgh
April ----

Father,

I never realized the country was so large or that it had so many people. I have heard endless tales of woe and seen as many. One thing I know; our little tragedy is a trifle in the larger scheme. What do we count when you look at the stars! We are all ants! I bear no grudge. I hope time and distance have softened you. We have nothing to gain from hatred. When I return (and I shall), let us plan to be pals. We are grown men and cannot afford to let life twist us. It is so short. We are mortal. I am the life of the party. I am a real swashbuckling type. I think you would like me now.

Your (devoted) son,
Pauli Svaboda

Omaha, Neb.
March ----

Mother,
Forgive me. I have become a Zionist. Israel needs me.

Tyrone

Miami Beach
September ----

Darling Daddy,
I wear my pants in the cutest way now. You would love it. Southern men are *not*, repeat are *not*, perfect gentlemen. They *take* their pleasures where they find them, and I can tell you very confidentially that they find them in

Your son,
(Who is) Murial

Miami Beach
September ----

Dearest Mumsie,

I feel that I really know you now. I am having an absolutely fab time on the beach here. It's the season, you know. The boys are gorgeous and very well stacked. I'm afraid I'm a little dissolute. Sometimes I'm out till daylight. It's amazing the money people will give little old me. I spend it all, naturally. Clothes and things. I've begun seeing a hairdresser. Marvelous! Please tell me how to handle the rough ones. And do think of me as

(Murial)

Omaha
April ----
Miami Beach
Sept. ----

Mother,

I'll write you from Israel. (I'm thinking of getting circumcised.)

Tyrone

PS: I forgot to mail this.

Miami Beach
Sept. ----

Mummie Dear,

Ignore my Omaha card. Why go to Israel? There's work to be done here! Besides, darling, what would the Pope think?

M.

Airdale, Mich.
Nov. ----

Dear Mother,
    I wish I were with you.

Your son,
X

Fort Smith, Ark.
January ----

Dear Father,
    Kronka says, "Dere's de cunt." He is big. He is strong. He takes care of me. Die.

Your son,
X

Brute Neighbor

AS YOU CAN SEE, MY LETTERS AND CARDS REVEAL AN IDIOT youth. There were more, but I have forgotten them. Of course I'm lying. I know them all. I was slow to mature. I learned little, in spite of my travels. I did not arrive at McCoomb Street immediately after leaving the junk yard. It took several years, during which I indulged in great wickedness. I became very sick and nearly died. My head swelled up and I saw wiggly worms in my stool. Old Pete left a deep impression on me. I often wondered what he would have thought of my depraved adventures. Especially my days on skid row. I became a wino there and did anything for a drink. Let me have this one reservation: I shall not tell you how low I sank. But it was there I met Dr. Vespucci, and he gave me the courage to go the last lap. I had confided my hopes and fears to him. Vespucci was, I think, a weak man to begin with. He had been married; he had three daughters; he had made good money working in a small medical group. He worked with numbers instead of names. One day he got the numbers mixed up and gave everybody the wrong treatment. He was terrified. But no one complained. He laughed himself silly. He tried it again with the same result. Finally he merely shuffled the numbers each day. It was faster. He got a reputation and made more money. Soon he went to work for R.I.B. as a senior specialist. He did everything in seventeen copies. He was an artist with his file boxes, a magician, a genius, a god. A few people died, many were surprised, but the averages worked out about the same as usual. If he operated in the wrong place, removed a lung instead of a kidney, he brazoned it out. Very often the patient thanked him profusely for his sharpness in detecting the real source of his trouble. He began to apply the principle elsewhere in his life and became a pillar of the community. He was invited to Washington and the most beautiful matrons threw themselves on his examining table. He realized that he had penetrated the riddle of the universe. And all the time he was laughing himself silly. His laughter began to intrude on his professional life. He laughed when he was consulted, he laughed in the hospital corridors, he laughed when he operated, he laughed when a patient died. ("Bugged out, eh?") He could not stop it. It came up from the ground, through his body, and out his mouth. One night he was kissing his wife's nipple, hardly able to contain his laughter, and he saw written across it the number 1642. He got up, dressed, left, and never returned. On Skid Row he did not laugh. He was happy. But enough about my past, enough about Vespucci. He was a philosopher and a great man. He told me where to go. The only point to be observed about my hegira is that I solved nothing. There was still a ghost at my back. I still had not faced truth. That was why I went to McCoomb Street. What is truth anyway? I've told you about my ablutions before the mirror. Did they help? I don't know. I think they *prepared* me, just as Melinda did. Ah, Melinda, I have the strangest feeling that she belongs here, to me. She will be back because she was right. I *am* an impresario, I have created something. I have sponsored a grotesque fact into being. I have put something in motion that will end as sheer spectacle. I know it, I feel it. Mrs. Maldive is already rehearsing some malignant finale. Why else does she avoid me? Is she changing her tactics? Trying to weaken my defenses? Where is she? There are things happening on my floor. I hear doors opening and shutting with greater frequency. Is my neighbor out of work? Did he ever work? Who is he? What does he look like? For many weeks I would not go out of my room except for the readings. I would empty my chamber pot at the same time. The first sign that all was not well was the razor. It was a little rusty along the edges, but still deadly. It leaned exactly on the part of the brush I used to stir the toilet bowl. Had my neighbor's resentment finally reached fever pitch? Was this a warning? For nearly seven years I had lived in relative peace. I had pursued the search for self slowly but methodically. I had sensed progress. Now I was wavering in my faith. I was frightened. I felt vulnerable to insights that would kill me. I was nervous. I slept often through sunrise. I no longer studied the quilt. If I had not had my readings I should have gone mad. Perhaps I am mad. Melinda. There was something wrong there. Why had I been so cruel? Did the end justify it? Where was she? When would she return? She was like the sun, the moon, the stars. She was heaven. I wept often over her blood on the floor. I was cold, abandoned. The fiend downstairs was hatching something diabolical. I know it, I was positive. And now the razor, the rusty razor. What did it mean? I became a whimpering mass and knew that soon I should be struck down. My sense of destiny saved me. It would be too great a loss to succumb before I had reached that point in life to which fate had assigned me. But then I must act, I must do something. I planned, I conserved my energy. I would open my door at twelve noon each day and look up and down the hall quickly. That might do it. When one has reduced life to simple repetitious components, it does not take much to shake the whole of it up. Even without routine, simple acts alter the universe. It is frightening. There is no control. But I was lucky. No, not lucky, wise. I had created my own universe, and I would disturb it only in ways I could measure. The ripples would not become waves and drown me. I would open my door exactly twelve inches on the stroke of noon, look one second in each direction, and then slam and bolt the door. That would be sufficient to undermine any conspiracy. I put my plan into effect and carried it out without incident for nine weeks. Nothing happened! My anxiety increased. I dared not go too far. I should be overwhelmed. My neighbor's door opened and closed during the hours of the night. Did he stand outside my door? Was he human? What did he want? I was afraid even to listen at the door. What would his breathing be like? Grating? Soft? With a wheeze? Should I hear his heart? I cowered in my bed. Suddenly things took a radical turn for the worse. I realize in retrospect that the initiative had been neatly taken out of my hands. Each morning when I went to the bathroom I naturally glanced at my neighbor's door. A simple precaution. Sensible. It was always closed. And then one morning it was not. It was open an inch. I stopped dead in my tracks, my throat was dry. My heart pounded. He couldn't be in the bathroom! Not during *my* hour! But the bathroom door was open also. Was he there, waiting? Was he standing behind the door with his rusty razor? Ready to slit my throat, expose my entrails, detach my testicles? I was, for a few seconds, stuck to the floor. I spilled some of my chamber pot fluid. It roused me from my frozen terror. I put the pot down and walked to my neighbor's door and listened—Nothing. I heard nothing. I could see only a little of one wall. It was covered with hieroglyphs, scribblings which I could not read. What kind of cultists lived there, what devotee, what fanatical Parsee? I retreated to my pot and thence to my readings. They were bad. I could see catastrophe, disaster. The next day I was eager for my hour. I could not realize how I had been trapped. When I entered the hall, I saw his door was open two inches. And the next day three. At last it was open enough for me to enter. The idea was one I would have shrunk from in the greatest fear only two months earlier. Now I felt curiosity, a *compulsion* to go in. I think it must have been something like the fascination of the condemned for the guillotine, the gallows, the electric chair, as if familiarity will render it less harmful. I pushed through the opening. There was no one there. I regained my breath and looked around the room. There was a calendar on one wall, many years old, a bed and a bureau. Nothing else. It was bare. Except for the writing, of course. In every color, large and small, print and script, one word over and over. I read it: EMMA. Suddenly I felt tears in my eyes. I wept profusely and did not know why! And then a door slammed. My heart jumped. The pounding was too sudden for my head. I thought it would crack. I rushed to my room, locked the door, and collapsed on the bed. Hours later, when I awoke, I realized my cheek was resting on something cold. It was a rusty razor. I thought of killing myself. It was unbearable, inhuman, what I was suffering. If it had been something in the open, something I knew and could see, I could face it. But this was unknown. I began to feel very sick from that time on. My insides wanted to come out. I could get no air. I was being crushed by some devilish grace. But at least I knew more. There was a woman involved. The man was clearly in love with her. That explained the doors. Lovers are always closing doors. But did it explain the razor? It did not. Unless—could he be jealous? Did he think I was in love with the same girl? Suddenly a monstrous idea flashed across my mind. Melinda! It was Melinda he loved! It was Melinda who visited his room! But why, then, did he have EMMA written on his walls? I became feverish. I had to know. I did not sleep the whole night. I heard the steady scratching on my door, as if someone were very patiently digging. I lay curled up in a corner of my bed. Impatiently I awaited the dawn, then the sun. My hour came at last. I opened the door. Yes, his door was wide open. Without the slightest hesitation I rushed in like a sinner to the confession box. I went to the bureau. I pulled out the drawers. They all contained the same thing. I laughed madly. "EMMA MALDIVE! EMMA MALDIVE!" I shrieked, shaking from laughter and relief. The drawers were full of Mrs. Maldive's used menstrual napkins! I ran back to my room still laughing. I saw it all now. I had inadvertantly promoted a romance between them by refusing to clean the toilet bowl! Thus is love sometimes born! And now she was making him the instrument of her vengeance. He was to destroy me for love of her! At least it was in the open. At last I could set up my defenses. But I could not, it turned out, have been more wrong. I was quite correct in assessing my danger. Mrs. Maldive had turned my neighbor into a deadly enemy. I saw one easy solution, of course. I could succumb, take Mrs. Maldive into my arms and whisper sweet words into her hairy ears. It was what she wanted above all. But if that surrender were not forthcoming, she would unleash her demented paramour on me. *Oh, folly! Last night I saw what fools we all were. I saw that we were pawns of a much larger game.* Mrs. Maldive holds my life in her hands. Yes. She will come for it soon. I know that. But I, too, hold her life in mine. And together we are being mangled by invisible fingers. For our sins, no doubt, our arrogance, our lusts. It was very late when I heard him there. I had courage because I knew what her devilish plan was. I crept to the door and looked through the keyhole. I saw blackness. I am convinced that is all we ever see. Then, as if he knew of my blindness, he lit a match. Or was it some God who did so? It doesn't matter. I saw. Against the coarse material an arthritic hand, and clenched in the hand *the long knife*. I saw it and screamed. And my scream stopped my heart. I saw blackness again. After my eyes had opened I lay there a long while. The sun rose. *I remembered everything!* Kronka's death no longer haunted me. I felt a strange peace, even though I was so close to violent dissolution. I had seen truth, or enough of it, at last. But more, I had lost my colossal vanity, my epic pride. If I could I would have prayed. I would have rejoiced in my ignorance and weakness. I would have laughed at my pretensions. I would have smashed my mirror into a million pieces. But I could not. I had one more trial to face. It would decide all. I knew that Mrs. Maldive would come. I knew that I owed her my life. I knew that she would come naked, dripping in her sweaty craving, and knock on my door. And behind another door I knew he whom I had so long hated would be standing with that knife which I knew so well. I would open the door and fall on my knees before her bloated mass, pierced by two black beads of long denied lust, slashed with her unholy orifice, and undulating in every fetid fold. Would she have a tail? Would she know me? Only she could save me. Did I dare to promise her long lost Melinda? Would I find only the ultimate madness in her embrace? I could only try. Perhaps her kiss will awaken me to my lost youth, and we shall all love. "Mother!" I shall say, "I've come home! Don't let him kill me!" The rest will be up to God.

Epilog

A FEW MORE WORDS ARE NECESSARY, I FIND, ALTHOUGH IT IS difficult to write. I am constrained. Sixteen hours have passed. Nothing has really changed. *Nothing.* Twice I have felt the sharp edge at my throat. It may be that we are in purgatory. I don't know. I can't understand it. I can't explain it. I feel sickeningly vulnerable. All my organs are exposed to a cold wind. A few words have passed between us, but garbled, incoherent, primitive like the first sounds of naked man. I am strangely moved even though frightened. Mrs. Maldive (Do I dare to utter the word "mother"?) has been holding me. Yes. Down there. She looks confused. Her teeth are like loose marbles in her mouth. I hear them rolling and rubbing one another. I am trying desperately to interpret sounds. I am convinced she wants me to believe she has never been above me, in the attic. She says it was God. That is absurd. I cannot believe that God looks like a walrus. Whatever was up there lusted for me monstrously. Of that I am certain. I have misunderstood her. She is perhaps mad. But if He is a walrus, perhaps that explains our predicament. Perhaps we are all walruses without knowing it. It is getting dark. I need rest, respite. I need comfort. Melinda will soon be here. I don't know how I know, but I can feel her coming. Will she be jealous? What can we say to one another? We have been shaped, we have been used. Can we complain? To what purpose? To whom? It has been our drama. All that matters now is that we shall be here, together again, in the dark, in the dark. We shall have to smell and know fingers. We shall have to draw close and rub flesh for warmth. Can we bear it? What will happen? Is that the form of death? Shall we tremble together and kill each other from fear? I feel nauseous. The light is going. I cannot see. There are sounds. There is movement. I am caught up in it. I—